ALEX

Band of Bachelors

Book 2

SHARON HAMILTON

BOOKS BY SHARON HAMILTON

SEAL BROTHERHOOD
SEAL Encounter (Book .5)
Accidental SEAL (Book 1)
SEAL Endeavor (Book 1.5)
Fallen SEAL Legacy (Book 2)
SEAL Under Covers (Book 3)
SEAL The Deal (Book 4)
Cruisin' For A SEAL (Book 5)
SEAL My Destiny (Book 6)
SEAL Of My Heart (Book 7)

BAD BOYS OF SEAL TEAM 3
SEAL's Promise (Book 1)
SEAL My Home (Book 2)
SEAL's Code (Book 3)

BAND OF BACHELORS
Lucas (Book 1)
Alex (Book 2)

TRUE BLUE SEALS
True Navy Blue (prequel to Zak)
Zak

ABOUT THE BOOK

Adrenaline junkie and Navy SEAL Alex Kowicki is one of four bachelor SEALs trying to navigate his successful military career while achieving his goals as a first class connoisseur of beautiful women. He isn't ready to jump back into anything but his free falls, HALO drops or his missions overseas. He trusts his buddies to fix him up with another blind date that won't be as dangerous as his last ones.

But Sydney Robinson has other plans. A beach volleyball player who can spike better than most men, and block with explosive speed to defend her side of the net, she executes a series of events to include stalking the handsome SEAL all the way to Sonoma County wine country, and delivering his carcass to her bed. Having achieved her first goal, she sets about to become a pro AVP player.

When duty calls and Alex is pulled back to Iraq to complete a failed mission, neither expects to find that the real danger is lurking very much close to home. But this fight might cost one of them their lives.

AUTHOR'S NOTE

I always dedicate my SEAL Brotherhood books to the brave men and women who defend our shores and keep us safe. Without their sacrifice, and that of their families—because a warrior's fight always includes his or her family—I wouldn't have the freedom and opportunity to make a living writing these stories. They sometimes pay the ultimate price so we can debate, argue, go have coffee with friends, raise our children and see them have children of their own.

One of my favorite tributes to warriors resides on many memorials, including one I saw honoring the fallen of WWII on an island in the Pacific:

> "When you go home
> Tell them of us, and say
> For your tomorrow,
> We gave our today."

These are my stories created out of my own imagination. Anything that is inaccurately portrayed is either my mistake, or done intentionally to disguise something I might have overheard over a beer or in the corner of one of the hangouts along the Coronado Strand.

I support two main charities: Navy SEAL/UDT Museum in Ft. Pierce, Florida. Please learn about this wonderful museum, all run by active and former SEALs and their friends and families, and who rely on public support, not that of the U.S. Government.

www.navysealmuseum.org

IF YOU GOT ANY CLOSER, YOU WOULD HAVE TO ENLIST

I also support Wounded Warriors, who tirelessly bring together the warrior as well as the family members who are just learning to deal with their soldier's condition and have nowhere to turn. It is a long path to becoming well, but I've seen first-hand what this organization does for its warriors and the families who love them. Please give what your heart tells you is right. If you cannot give, volunteer at one of the many service centers all over the United States. Get involved. Do something meaningful for someone who gave so much of themselves, to families who have paid the price for your freedom. You'll find a family there unlike any other on the planet.

www.woundedwarriorproject.org

**Go here for an audio snippet for
Band of Bachelors: Alex.**

soundcloud.com/sharon-hamilton-1/band-of-
bachelors-alex-sydney-sleeping

CHAPTER 1

ALEX KOWICKI LIKED blind dates, *in a fucked up kind of way,* he thought to himself. It was an opinion shared by his housemates—other bachelor members of his SEAL Team. It was considered a sport, seeing who they could rig him up with and how he would escape.

"Sort of self-preservation. If we don't get you good and laid, we can't play with you," Jake told him yesterday. He was one of Alex's roommates in the now-infamous bachelor pad overlooking the bay.

"We live vicariously through you and all your sexcapades," Thomas added. The SEAL explosives expert was halfway in and out of his own house. The divorce was not quite final so there was survivor guilt and make-up sex all over the place. The men were taking bets which way it would turn out.

Alex was amped with more than his usual dose of excitement today. He was almost manic. The timing for this was good—too good. He would be leaving early

Sunday morning to drive up to Sonoma County with Lucas and several others to help Nick and Devon with the winery. But there was discussion amongst the group about perhaps purchasing some land and doing an all-SEAL winery too.

This was going to be his usual Friday night blind date, which meant he could woo the little lady all night—and all day Saturday if she was spectacular. And if not, well, he could get out of Dodge and wouldn't be back for over a week. It also saved the hassle he knew girls went through waiting for a callback from him. If he was leaving, there was no expectation of a return call. The pressure was off!

He was full of expectation, as if his life was about to change forever.

They didn't tell him anything about her, except for the fact that she was tall. Really, really tall. They always said that with a smile when describing her to him, so he was prepared for a lady maybe six feet in height. He loved tall, long-legged girls who liked to wear those Jesus sandals that laced nearly up to their Holy of Holies. He was praying for the chance, just once, to be able to untie one of those types of sandals and have the tiny leather shoelace be so close to her crotch the backs of his hands would be singed from the proximate distance to her heat. An easy couple of millimeters to go, and he'd hit pay dirt. The angels would sing.

Alex was getting hard just thinking about it. When he woke up this morning with a boner, it interfered with his early skydive. Jumping out of an airplane would take the edge off his nerves, he thought, but he wasn't that lucky and nearly did a three-point landing like a tripod on the moon.

Her name was Sydney, they'd told him yesterday. He immediately asked them if she was a virgin, because that was always a game-stopper.

"Hell no," Jake had said. "You think I'd put a virgin babe in your hands, you asshole?"

"Gee, thought we were buds. What about *my* feelings?" he'd feigned a whine to one of the bachelor SEALs he cohabited with. The other SEAL wives and girlfriends used the term "domicile" in quotes. It was more a crash pad. Raunchy posters of darkly-greased women in torn T-shirts and thong panties adorned their apartment walls, conjuring up visions of writhing around on an auto body shop floor. Several days' worth of cereal bowls and coffee mugs waited until the number of their cousins in the cabinet diminished to zero before being allowed a proper bath in detergent, meanwhile hosting a variety of life forms with white or dark green fuzzy outlines. The smell of sweat always present, like the elixir of life it was. It was the way they measured the worth of everything: the more sweat, the better it was for all concerned.

"Your hurt feelings? You'll heal, Alex. And if you don't, who the fuck cares?"

Well, true enough.

The fact that this blind date made Alex super excited didn't bode well for the encounter. Usually when they seemed too good to be true, they were. Disaster could be looming right around the corner. He didn't doubt he would let himself go all double-SEAL on her, make it difficult for her to walk afterwards, which was the kind of fun he was, quite frankly, hoping for. He chalked up his reservations to age. Still, at nearly thirty, he was one of the old guys on the Team. Old in terms of tours as well as marriages. Only one of those marriages counted legally, but that one was bad enough.

He wasn't about to do what his friend Lucas had done—gotten himself tied up with a hottie before the divorce papers were signed. It would have been way smarter, not to mention way less of a negative adventure on Lucas's kids and everyone else on the Team, if he could have parted with Connie before he started round two. Alex had been smart enough not to make that mistake at least. But it had been said before, some SEALs feared being alone. Alex knew Lucas was one of those. He wondered if he might be the same.

Alex had gotten seriously in lust with Brandy, the buxom waitress at the Pink Bunny bar in Coronado, who gave head he was ashamed to admit he loved better than sex. So he and Ryan had married their ladies in a double wedding ceremony presided over by Elvis one evening in Vegas. He barely remembered that night, each SEAL drawing energy off the other in what could only be seen as a mercy mission to the Love Boat of Eternal Bliss. Oddly enough, that was the name of the chapel: Eternal Bliss. He'd told Ryan it sounded more like a funeral parlor. In a way, it was.

His marriage lasted three months, but his boners hadn't stopped every time he thought about Brandy. Her attractive smile was not her best feature and was often overlooked by the SEALs Alex hung around with. She also lacked domestic ability, except in the bedroom.

Brandy didn't get pregnant like Ryan's wife did, yet Alex knew he was the lucky one. Not that he would have minded being permanently connected to Brandy no matter what she wound up doing with her life. He loved kids and knew one day he'd make one hell of a father. He wasn't littering the globe with children like Jake had done. But having a couple little Alex urchins, well, it was something he'd like to do. Not now, of course.

Women think this way.

He was one of those guys who would love the kids and put up with the wife.

The last date had been with a personal trainer and

martial arts expert. But she'd neglected to tell him she frequented the bondage bars in San Diego and was into women as much as she was men, especially women who liked to get tied up. He should have known better when she actually dug the posters and promised him she'd give him some of her personal collection to enhance his room. She didn't have room for them at her own place.

Alex's sister was a nun, which he took as a sign God was watching out for his mother after all the crap he'd put her through growing up. But that still left one unresolved score to settle: there were no grandkids. Talk about not caring who he married! She just wanted grandkids around, and heck, she'd even raise them if he'd let her.

"Don't have to fall in love. Just find someone who will raise your spawn, and I'll do all the rest."

Good old Mom. She'd even picked up on Alex's language, much to the horror of Joanne, his sister. Alex nicknamed his sister *Joan* after the famous one. And, of all things, *Joan* was a pacifist. Only good thing about that was there was little chance any of his Team buds would ever get their hands on her. One less woman to defend, and that was indeed a very good thing.

Alex showered and began to shave, then considered going with the stubble for the bad boy look he liked. His dark features against his naturally pale skin made him resemble a vampire or evil dark angel of the underworld, he thought. He could look like a choirboy one minute, and the next, he swore his eyes glowed red, judging from the reaction he occasionally got.

When he arrived at the Rusty Scupper for fortification before meeting Sydney, he expected some of his SEAL buddies to have brought their wives or girlfriends too. But no, as Alex sauntered in and took his seat amongst the clean-shaven group, he picked up he was to be the evening's entertainment.

Whistles filled the room. Jake started with the evening's insults and smack talk. "Look at you all duded out. You look like a college kid."

"Alex, you going for a job interview or something?" joked Thomas.

"A funeral. It's gotta be a funeral," Carter added.

"Shut the fuck up." Alex studied the small group in front of him. "Hey, I thought this was to be a coed, group thing," he scowled at Jake, Thomas, Jones, and Carter.

"Still could be, if you want," Carter quipped. Alex narrowed his eyes suspiciously at the African-American SEAL's offhand behavior and the way he sought out grins from the other bachelor Team members.

After the chuckles died down, Alex barked like he was giving his LPO's orders. "So I want to see a show of hands who's met her."

Only Jake raised his hand. "But only from afar."

Alex grabbed his chin at the perfect angle, cracking his neck so loud that one of the patrons at the bar whipped around on his stool. Though Alex's neck felt better, his spine was stiff, his butt cheeks were tight, and the backs of his thighs locked up. He had to take a pee.

"Jake, you keep her company if she arrives early while I go pee, will ya?" He wanted to sound casual, but knew he failed when the little conference guffawed behind him.

The bathroom was plastered with Polaroid pictures of vehicles and brothers-in-arms, some with faces cut out. One had been varnished into the wall because the picture had been stolen so many times. There was the meek-looking Saddam Hussein in handcuffs and orange jump suit, his hair going in all directions like a homeless man's. It had been taken soon after being captured and before his execution. It existed so no one got it wrong what this place was, who frequented it, or who the real heroes were. Alex wondered how many other men gave this picture the three-finger salute every time they pulled their dick out to pee like he was doing now.

Returning to the table of SEALs from Team 3, he took up a seat next to Jake.

"So tell me about her."

"We were coming in from a swim and found her on the beach," said Jake.

"You and who?"

"None of these guys. They'd give you way more than I'm going to if they'd met her, trust me," Jake said, pointing at the other faces at the table. "I was with Coop, Kyle, Danny and Zak. Not an official swim. Working with Zak, you know?"

They didn't laugh this time. Everyone was pulling for Zak, who had lost an eye from an assassin's ricocheted round and was working hard to make a place back on Team 3. Alex had been injured in the same attack, but his were only scars. Zak had lost much more. Again, Alex was feeling lucky.

"So what's wrong with her?" Alex inquired.

Jake leaned back and gave him the Cheshire Cat grin of the century, showing off his pearly whites, his blue eyes sparkling in the low light. When Jake slapped Alex on the back, he nearly dropped his beer.

"Not a damned thing, my man. Not a fuckin' damned thing."

Alex was hard all of a sudden. Last weekend had become a long time ago for his usually nightly booty worship exercise. He looked from Carter to Jones, then around to Thomas and back at Jake. "You're full of shit."

The whoops and hollers began in earnest. Alex let their voices fade as he tended to the burgeoning in his pants. He talked to himself like an older brother. *Don't get your hopes up. Remember, one man's babe is another man's nightmare. You're leaving the day after tomorrow to go up to Sonoma County, and you'll never see this girl again for the rest of your life.*

It was the ideal set up for a casual and nearly anonymous date.

But something was wrong. Something was grossly different, like he was being led with golden chains to some kind of hot female house of pain. It scared him, but it also excited him more than he wanted to admit. Jake's words—*Not a fuckin' thing*—crawled around his brain like a black cat in heat. The rest of his beer was gone. He ordered another. His ears buzzed as the happy banter flew back and forth. The legendary smack talk they all did made muffled, unintelligible background noise.

He tapped his lace-up, lightweight Oxfords. His normal cargo pants and canvas slip-ons were back at the apartment. Today, he wore his faded Levis and a long-sleeved shirt.

Holy fuck.

His button down shirt was yellow! Now, what kind of a message was he sending the guys and the lady he was about to meet?

Better than a fuckin' pink shirt.

He sat back, closed his eyes, and raised his forehead to the ceiling, composing himself like when he used to pray. As he settled his jaw and made a small adjustment to his shoulders, he opened his eyes.

For a second, he could have sworn Coop's six-foot-four frame had blocked the sunlight at the entrance to the Scupper, like he'd seen a hundred times. But as he looked closer at the shape, he noticed a slim waist, curvy thighs, and a gait that was nothing like their tall medic, Calvin "Coop" Cooper. She nearly had to duck to get through the doorway, which meant she was no six-foot lady.

She was probably *taller* than Coop.

She headed right for him as if she'd known him her whole life, like she was following a tractor beam to the Death Star. He'd seen girls with radar for SEALs. This one was honed and toned and on a mission. Her shirt must have been made for an eight-year-old, but her forty-something at least D bra size was bulging for release. He clearly saw ten inches of tanned midriff, and it was all muscle.

As he remembered himself and brought his body to stand, he noticed she wore sandals with leather straps crisscrossing up her shapely calves, over her knees, and disappearing under her incredibly short jeans skirt.

He was weaving. The snickering at the table

brought him to attention, and he stood erect, in every way he was capable. She looked right at his crotch and smiled.

"You must be Alex."

"You must be Sydney."

"I am." Her voice was husky and sultry. Alex's usual casual demeanor and smooth-as-glass countenance under pressure evaporated. "Been waiting to meet you all day, Alex."

He knew if he shook her hand it would be the end of something. Maybe his dignity.

He did it anyway.

CHAPTER 2

SYDNEY LIKED THE feel of the SEAL's hands. She also felt the adrenaline pulsing through his veins. He was good at control, which she liked as well. His hands were callused, verifying he was indeed a SEAL and not a poser. She even liked the fact that his voice broke when he spoke to her for the first time.

Alex looked good, really good.

The country music at the bar and the low-level sports channels on the three big screen TVs overhead, the occasional laughter and male banter faded into background noise. She could have been standing in the middle of a men's locker room. The view was that nice.

She slipped her hand from his as he held on just a tad longer than he probably meant to. Scanning the table, they had not made room for her, so she looked up, and before she could ask the question, Alex offered her the head of the table, standing behind her chair.

"A gentleman," she purred so softly she wasn't sure

he could hear her, and took a seat. His hands gripped her shoulders briefly before he took his place perpendicular. "Hi, fellas," she waved to the table and got muffled acknowledgements back. "So Alex, this is a group thing, then?" She knew it wasn't, but couldn't resist the poke at his expense.

One of his friends was laughing. At Alex. She didn't take it as a sign of any disrespect to her. Alex sported a bashful grin and was nodding.

Did that mean she'd passed the test? She'd spent the whole afternoon getting waxed every place she could and getting her nails done in a white French manicure which matched her toes. They nearly glowed in the low light of the famous hangout.

She saw the pictures of young handsome men plastered over the walls above the liquor bottles, beneath the TVs. "Our Heroes" was hand written on a white sign that she'd seen over the years growing up in San Diego, when she and her high school girlfriends used to try to stop by and pick up a SEAL. They'd always gotten kicked out.

This time, they surrounded her.

Alex asked her what she wanted to drink, got the waitress' eye, and ordered her Merlot. "I'd share one with you, but I prefer beer."

"No problem. To each his own," she assured him. The chocolate brown of Alex's eyes and his dark hair made him look boyish and younger than he surely was. She'd been concerned she'd be older than him, but as she studied him she began to relax.

After she received her wine glass, they toasted the beer and the Merlot. "Here's to blind dates and…" Alex stumbled for what to say.

"How about just blind dates so we don't get ahead of ourselves?" she whispered.

When he smiled, she found the dimple at the right side of his full lips intoxicating. Her fingers itched to smooth over his jawline and feel the beginning stubble growing there already.

Sydney wasn't sure how long they'd been staring into each other's eyes, but the table began to clear out, and one by one the four other SEALs waved good-bye, winking and patting Alex on the back or socking his arm. She noted they horsed around like brothers in a very large family of boys.

"So, what do you do, Sydney?"

That's when she realized he'd not been told anything about her.

"I'm three years out of college, playing the beach volleyball circuit for now, looking to rack up enough wins to claim a good sponsor and an even better partner."

"Partner?"

"You've seen them play on the beach, I'll bet. Two

ladies. Lots of suntan lotion. Skimpy bathing suits and shades?"

"Oh yes. All over the place here."

"Southern California is big beach volleyball country. The best players in the world live here. All I need is one. My last partner tore her rotator cuff and will be out for months. We'd come to the end of our game anyway. Looking for a new partner, probably someone better than me." She watched his reaction. "If I can."

"Why better than you?"

"I won't get better playing with someone who isn't better than I am. I might have strengths my partner might not have. But I'm looking for someone who can set my spikes."

"As in hitting it back over the net?"

"Yes, so it will come at you at ninety miles per hour and land five feet or less from the net."

He was checking out his beer glass, in deep thought. "Not a whole lot of people could return that ball. I know I sure couldn't."

"Oh, I guarantee you couldn't." She followed it up with a smile when his eyes darted to meet hers. The challenge was on. The best part about dating someone new was learning where their hot spots were and then pressing them. She liked pushing her limits, but she liked pushing the limits of her dates even more. Funny thing was, she was reeling herself in. This was her being nice, and already she was alarming him with her intensity. But if he was sensitive, she needed to know that, and know it quick. No sense wasting time.

He recovered nicely. "So, how many times have you jumped out of an airplane?"

That was an excellent scene-changer. Ask me about something I've never done. Expose my weak spot. Well, good for you, sailor. Her follow-up to that move would be to pretend he nailed her. And then she'd finish him off.

"Never." She didn't let up on him, staring him full in the face. She gave him the innocent shrug and puppy dog eyes. It worked.

"We'll have to fix that sometime." He winced, almost imperceptibly, perhaps second-guessing his words.

"I like fixing things."

"I'll bet you do." His low, rumbling cadence sent her blood pumping. He wouldn't look at her anymore, but he smiled, knowing she was watching him, telling her he didn't mind the scrutiny. Yes, he could handle the heat, she thought. He'd do just fine.

He was one of the handsomest men she'd ever seen. His shoulders and arms were huge, barely fitting into the long-sleeved shirt he was wearing. Just by the way he sat, she could tell he wasn't used to dressing up. The jeans looked new and the shirt had been taken right out of a laundry box, the fold marks not pressed out.

"So you wanna go to a movie or something?" he asked.

"Sure. As long as it isn't a sad one."

"I hate mushy ones too." His chin wrinkled as he frowned, adding a slight inclination of his head. "What *do* you like?"

"My favorite? My very favorite movies?"

"Yes. Of the movies playing now. At the theater, as opposed to renting—"

"Zombies."

His eyes closed for a moment as he took in what she'd said. He licked his lips, leaned on his right arm, and studied her. "Really?"

"I love horror films."

"I'll be goddamned." Alex shook his head, casually perusing the room. Then he finished his beer, running his tongue over his lower lip again, and whispered with a sexy smile, "Let's go get you the bloodiest, creepiest zombie movie playing in the whole county then, Sydney. Would you like that?"

Her insides were cheering. He had no idea what he'd just said to her, a huge green light the size of the moon staring her in the face. The burning muscles in her thighs from today's workout were painful, but still felt good. She knew she'd be stiff when she stood, and stiffer still after a long movie. It was an admission price she was willingly going to pay.

"Yes," she returned, "I'd like that very much, Alex."

He hesitated a few seconds and then leaned across the table and whispered, "Well then, why don't you check your phone for movies and times, while I take a leak. Sound fair?"

"No problem." Sydney didn't look up as he walked to the rear of the Scupper. Within seconds she checked the movie times of the film she knew was opening this weekend. The theater was about a half hour away, and the movie started in forty minutes.

Tapping on the screen of her phone, the trailer began, showing white-faced flesh-eating monsters growling and drooling into the foreground. The dripping red movie title oozed down the length of the picture frame.

"The Zombie Rebel Alliance Returns," said the announcer. The last shot before the screen froze was a greenish-gray hand with flesh peeling from it, showing bones and cartilage, trying to reach out from the phone to grab her.

Perfect!

CHAPTER 3

$\mathbf{A}$LEX KNEW IT was a bad sign to be in the men's room twice before he and Sydney exited the Scupper, but his bladder was acting up. With the cups of coffee at the dive airport and the protein drink he'd had for breakfast, he guessed his liquid intake had been huge. He'd not been paying attention, and that was very unlike him.

He decided to confide in good old Saddam.

"You ever get nervous when you were dating way back when?" he asked as he began his stream, which relieved him immediately. The muscles in his lower belly relaxed and his back stopped hurting. "She likes horror films. Should I read anything into that?"

He didn't get a response from the sad photograph.

Sydney stood when he returned to their table, announcing, "Got the perfect one, but it starts soon. We gotta book." She'd put her jacket on, and slung her purse over her shoulder, looking like a little girl ready for an ice cream.

Alex studied the theater's address on her cell phone screen and nodded. "I was there last weekend." When he noticed she'd frowned, he assured her, "No worries, I haven't seen this one yet." Her eyes softened, but maintained their eager expression. "I guess we should leave your car here. Pick it up later?"

Her lips formed an "O" and then she licked them, her tongue brushing-over her bright red lipstick. Her sexy smile spread slowly, getting him dangerously close to being inappropriate. Teasing his self-control further, she smelled wonderful, the very definition of a woman heavily laden with pheromones. She was so damn kissable, he wanted to just take her in his arms and try to change her mind about the movie. But he also knew he wanted her primed and excited. Her energy was addicting, and for now, all he wanted to do was to get her good and stoked.

She lowered her eyes, giving him the ripe opportunity to gaze at her chest, which lusciously rose and fell with her heavy breathing. "My girlfriend dropped me off," she said as she raised her chin. "So I'm afraid I'm going to rely on you getting me home." Her eyelids fluttered just a tad as an exclamation mark he couldn't miss.

His pants were so damned tight, he worried the zipper would break. He'd thought it impossible he could get more aroused when she suddenly touched her forefinger to his lips and he found himself sucking her digit to beyond the first joint. Her eyes were transfixed with how he fed off her, devoured her essence. He reached for the back of her head, intending to run his fingers through her beautiful, honey-brown hair and pull her into him, but she stepped back.

He nearly gasped. Her eyes became dark, as she must have sensed his need, his total desire for this women he'd only spoken a few words to. It was indeed a chemical reaction he'd never felt before. His knees began to weaken. He realized she was waiting for him to speak, but he couldn't find his tongue, having nearly swallowed it.

In that way women do, she entangled her arm around his, drew him close to her body, and whispered, further binding him with the golden threads of enchantment and desire, "Let's not miss the movie, okay?"

THE THEATER'S THICK red carpeting had a gold scrolling pattern embedded in the fibers. The smell of popcorn made a trip to the snack bar a must, even though they were short on time.

"I'll have a quad latte," Sydney said to the tatted help behind the counter. The young lady attendant chewed on her bottom lip, rolling her tongue over her lip ring.

"Make that two," he interjected. "You like chocolate?"

Sydney lit up like a Christmas tree. "Absolutely! A food group."

She was perfectly formed, which indicated to Alex she only drank quad shots of espresso and munched down chocolate and popcorn on special occasions. He desperately hoped he was one of those.

She pointed to the boxes of chocolate covered mints, and as Alex was paying for them, she ripped open the box and dumped them into her popcorn. Then, she tossed the mixture like a gourmet salad. When she caught him staring at her, she stuck out her lower lip with the beginnings of a frown. "Don't tell me you're one of those guys who likes to separate his food and eats in a clockwise direction."

"Not a chance, Sydney."

She extended her arm as they ambled over to theater eleven. Alex carried the coffees while Sydney held the popcorn mixture. "I like the sweet and the salty together. Try it." She stopped like they had all the time in the world. He hadn't expected it, so gently ran into her body, which wasn't an unpleasant feeling. His brain practically groaned at the sensation of being pressed against her curves.

He allowed her to feed him a fingerful of popcorn

with one Junior Mint in the middle. Her eyes were transfixed on his lips again as she intently watched him eat and react to her concoction.

Alex had to admit, he liked the taste. He held her coffee while he took a chaser from his cup, watching her again. The familiar zing down his spine gladdened his spirits. He put his palm at the small of her back and gently led her into the darkened auditorium. She was putty at his touch and took his direction without resistance.

God, have I died and gone to Heaven?

The credits had just come on and the background music was eerie. Because of her height, Sydney adjusted herself lower in the cushioned seat. Alex hunkered down next to her, peering over the large box of popcorn. Her eyes looked scared at first as she focused on the film, filling her mouth with popcorn and the chocolate mints. He was fascinated just watching her eat.

He didn't want to stare at her the whole time so he tore his attention from her occasionally, but he doubted she noticed. The movie was big on loud, bloody screams, and Alex noted her eyes began to grow wider with every one.

At one point, a girl was franticly looking for a hiding spot from a male zombie and had decided to use the closet. But the whole audience knew the zombie was in that closet, waiting to attack.

"No!" Sydney shouted, which brought several heads in the theater turning abruptly. "Don't be stupid!" she followed.

Alex was nearly jerked from his seat at her outburst. Didn't she know it was only a movie?

"Shhh," he whispered, putting his arm around her shoulder. He could feel her blood pumping as her upper torso began to shake. He took that as a sign she needed the shelter of his arms, and he was only too happy to oblige. She ducked under his chin, pressing her breasts into his ribs so hard he could feel the lace of her bra.

Of course the male zombie tore the girl in the movie to shreds. This made Sydney hold onto him tighter, something Alex as grateful for. But when she grasped his dick and squeezed hard, he dropped his coffee with a loud "plunk."

Her expression was confusing, as the movie played in the background. He started to dip his head, hoping for a kiss that would lead to her releasing his balls, which now started to burn. But on the large screen, the hero arrived, using a large sword to slice off the top of the zombie's head, right above the ears. The view of the unfortunate zombie's putrid, dark green brain matter and deep maroon blood spurting caught Alex up short and he forgot the pain in his pants.

And then Sydney interrupted his confusion.

"Woot! Woot!" she screamed and air-fisted several times, releasing his balls.

By now, half the audience was mumbling. A few chuckles were sprinkled in as well. Sydney was unfazed. She was about to give another shout when the hero sliced the zombie in half at the torso, but Alex held his palm over her mouth.

"Shhhh, Syd. Quiet or they'll kick us out."

She threw his hand away, dropping her popcorn box. Using both hands, she climbed up on his lap, her leather laces cutting into her soft flesh, and drilled him a deep throat kiss. "Gawd, Alex, I'm so hot right now, I don't know what to do." She fumbled under her skirt, and then pushed his hand underneath.

Alex knew exactly what to do. And the audience wouldn't mind one bit.

"I'm taking you home."

"Fuck me, Alex."

The teens behind their seats were having a good time listening to their interaction. He heard one of them whisper, "I'm right here, baby. Come on over."

Alex glowered at the youths. He had been trying to come to his feet, grabbing her hand and yanking her up to a standing position. She had hold of his balls again.

"Fuck me, Alex," she repeated her plea, this time a little louder.

The audience was erupting with complaints, while he attempted to scoot in front of half a dozen people seated next to them. It was all he could do to keep his balance to avoid stepping on someone's toes, and at last he had to stop and remove her hand from his groin. His blood pressure was skyrocketing.

"Fuck sake, Sydney, keep your hands to yourself or—"

"Shhh!" came someone's loud reprimand.

He wanted to go punch the asshole who tried to shush him. Exhaling, he blurted out, "Okay, we're leaving. Leaving right now." It was loud enough so the whole room heard him.

Alex made huge strides down the side aisle, turning toward the exit. He could feel Sydney having difficulty keeping her balance as he tugged on her arm, her sandals doing chicken scratches on the concrete floor. Just as they descended the ramp to the exit door, someone shouted, "Have a good time you two!"

Fuckin' Christ. He didn't know whether to be upset, or just give her what she seemed to want, a very public screw on the well-padded, deep red floor of the theater lobby. But he knew this wasn't conduct becoming a Navy SEAL, and nothing was worth jeopardizing that. At least that part of his brain was functioning.

"Geez, Sydney. What's the matter with you?" He threw her hand down like a dirty rag.

At first she seemed taken aback. Then a deep furrow formed between her eyebrows. She tilted her head to the right as if she hadn't heard him properly.

"Horror films make me horny as hell. What can I say?" She shrugged. "I guess I should have warned you."

Alex took a step away from her and nearly ran into another couple rushing to enter the theatre. "Anything else I need to know?" he finally asked her.

He was dead serious, but she took it as a joke. It was no joke to him. His string of recent blind dates had him wary all of a sudden.

"Like whatever do you mean?" she answered, batting her big brown eyes.

"Like do you like to tie men up, that sort of shit? Because, sweetheart, I'm not into that. I once dated a girl—" His words were truncated by her palm, which quickly covered his mouth so hard it was nearly a slap.

"I don't want to know anything about that. Don't ever bring up other women again." Her voice was low and deep, bubbling with anger.

Holy shit. I just met her. Why didn't I see her as the nutjob she is?

He was going to seriously have words with the boys in his apartment who had set up this date. This was going to be the last time. He was done with these blind dates that were more a horror film than the one they'd just come from.

He valued his life and his career too much to risk it just for a piece of ass.

CHAPTER 4

SYDNEY KNEW SHE'D blown it with the SEAL.

You were going to take it slow. Get that little demon tied up and sent to the closet so she didn't act out inappropriately. She cursed herself for not working out harder today. That was the solution—that and staying away from caffeine and chocolate. But she couldn't help herself today.

She'd dated much older guys, even a couple of former SEALs, but it usually took four or five intense dates before they'd go flying on their way. That part she didn't mind. She was usually tired of them by then anyhow.

But this one was different. He had a mild, quiet manner about him, yet she could tell he could handle the crazy life, just didn't like it in his ladies. It was okay if he did stuff halfway around the world that any adventure-seeker would pine for. At home, he wanted to be surprised, but not blindsided.

And she'd blindsided him tonight. She came onto him without much of a warning. It was too strong, and now, perhaps, she'd lost him. She'd never get a chance to have a second date. Her over-the-knee leather laces were hurting her now. She couldn't wait to get them off.

They'd taken turns clearing their throats during his drive to her house, but no one spoke after she gave directions. He wasn't going to bring her to his apartment. He didn't have to explain it. That part was obvious.

What wasn't so obvious was why he was denying the chemistry they had between them. One taste of his tongue and all the toggles got flipped to full on. She was a starved animal, or a wounded animal protecting something. Maybe both.

What?

She tossed the thought out the window and tried to act like she wasn't disappointed, but the closer they got to her place, the sadder she felt.

"I'm sorry, Alex. Really sorry."

He nodded and chuckled in spite of himself. "You should come with a warning label."

"I don't know what came over me," she lied.

"Sweetheart, I think you had it all planned. You don't fool me one bit." His words were sharp and it hurt.

She was quiet, waiting for him to apologize. If she said something right now, the opportunity would be lost, maybe forever. At last, her silence paid off.

"Look, Sydney, I'm sorry, but I can't tell if you did this on purpose or just—"

She turned toward him, placing her knee on the bench seat of his Hummer. "Yes. I'm really that way. Horror films turn me on. The coffee, the popcorn and all that chocolate—all those things are triggers. I get horny just walking past a See's Candy Store. I can't watch movie trailers for zombie movies in mixed company. But I am sorry. And you're right, I should have told you."

He wasn't buying her explanation. He shook his head and mumbled something.

"Do my buddies know about all this?"

"Your buddies? What do your buddies have to do with this?"

"The guys who arranged the blind date."

"I don't remember meeting any of your friends. My girlfriend and I were playing at the beach. She told me she had someone she wanted me to meet. Since I am unattached, I was game. So I agreed."

"So the guys didn't talk to you?"

She found this to be really funny, throwing her head back in a full-throated laugh. "I talk to guys on the beach nearly every day. I play beach volleyball, or did you forget that about me?"

Alex didn't say anything else for a few minutes. The silence was killing her.

Then it hit her. He thought she was some kind of freak. Well, he was partly right. As long as she exercised she could keep the crazy thoughts from overtaking her. She worked out and played hard, harder than most men. She knew she could take down most of them or handle herself in a dark alley. Physical contact didn't scare her at all.

But Alex thought she was a freak. This made her mad.

He pulled up to her bungalow. Her roommate's car wasn't in the driveway, which would have been a good thing if their relationship was going any further, but she noted it without celebration.

When he stopped the truck, she opened the door and hopped out, headed straight for her front door without waving good-bye or saying a word. The sooner she could get to that hot shower and then her well-lubed vibrator, the better. She didn't need a man to get off. But she had to get off.

"Hey," she heard him shout. She pivoted on her heels and saw him standing outside the driver door. "You just going to walk off like that, not say a word? What kind of manners is that?"

"I thought you made it perfectly clear, or have you

changed your mind?"

"Changed my mind?"

"About fucking me."

He swore and shook his head. He was laughing when his gaze met hers a few seconds later. "Christ, Sydney. Are you okay? I mean, I've never met anyone like you before."

"And I'm supposed to do what with that?"

"No, it's just a manner of—"

"In case you hadn't noticed, I'm tanked up, ready for a hot shower and some hotter sex with my devices than I'll ever get out of you. No reason to put a bow tie on the fact that we're incompatible."

His square jaw and stern glare showed her some intensity she really liked. She'd picked a scab. He was angry.

Serves you right.

She turned and didn't check out the slam of the truck door behind her. But she did note that the engine had been turned off, and then there were the footsteps that got closer until she felt the tug on her arm. Before she could protest, he had her in a lip-lock, sucking her tongue into his mouth as one hand found its way to her panties under her skirt.

"Sydney, we might be totally incompatible, but can't we still fuck?"

Hallelujah.

She checked to see if any of her nosey neighbors were peering out their windows. They were used to watching her parade her trophies up and down the front walkway.

"Well, sailor," she said before he could plunge his tongue down her throat again. "that's more like it."

His hands were all over her ass while she unlocked her front door. He didn't spend any time looking at all the sports posters on the walls, the pictures of her on the cover of Sports Illustrated, or the trophies overflowing from her bedroom, burdening the living room bookshelf devoid of books. She checked for a note from Carole and found it taped to the mirror.

Be back in the morning.

They had this rule, if one of them was going to be gone all night, to let the other one know.

Alex bent her over the hallway chest, urgently pulling her panties down over her trussed thighs to her knees. His hand accepted the gift of her breast as she was pressed forward onto it. Her nipples were taught and ached, especially after he began pinching them. She groaned, spread her knees further, and raised her tailbone, rubbing her sex against the front of his jeans. She heard the zipper and then the drop of his pants.

"Honey, you got something?"

"I'm on the pill."

"Is that enough?" He kissed her neck.

"God, I hope so. You—you want to wait?"

"It would be smarter." But she could tell he was unconvinced.

"I don't sleep around, Alex." He was trying not to, but she could feel the tip of his cock brushing against her butt cheek.

He backed away for a second. "I do. But I'm always careful. I just wasn't prepared, and I'm so sorry about that."

She sighed. "Thank you, Alex. But I can't wait. Please…"

His low growl at the back of her neck sent chills down her spine. The warmth of his body pressed into her, as one arm wrapped around her waist. He spread her cheeks, letting a finger slip inside her core just before he rammed his cock inside her.

"You like that, baby?"

"Yes," she answered breathlessly. He took up a slow, deep rhythm, his hips undulating in a circular motion. He was getting harder. "You gonna let me come?" she finally found the words to say.

He didn't stop his thrusting as he raised her with his thighs underneath hers so that she was pinned on him and perfectly balanced.

"Nuh-uh. Not this time, sweetheart."

"I like it when I come first."

"I do too, but, baby, don't make me stop. I'm like

you were at the theater, I want to fuck you senseless. Maybe next time?" His breath hitched as he groaned. She could feel his release was eminent.

She quickly whipped her body around and fell to her knees in front of him, putting her lips on his glistening member. She curled her tongue over him, sucked, and then ran her teeth over his head.

He appeared to be in shock at what she'd done, but powerless to do anything about it. His climax was overcoming him quickly. His cock began to spasm as she felt the warm come spurt down her throat. She inhaled deep, and pulled him down her throat, sucking up his balls too.

Alex was gasping as he gripped the chest top and struggled to stay on his feet. Sydney's hands scratched his buttocks and then squeezed his flesh until he started to scream.

"Wait!" he shouted.

She couldn't talk because he was totally filling her mouth, but she relinquished her hold on his ass. Her fingers feathered his butt cheeks as she drew her elbows together and squeezed her tits on either side of his left thigh until they hurt. He attempted to go deeper down her throat until his spill was complete.

She teased his cock as he began to withdraw, curling her tongue up and down his shaft, kissing and licking his underside in long strokes. He held her head with palms over her ears, and then let his fingers lace through her hair, pulling her onto him further, before releasing her.

"God, Sydney, I've never—"

"Shush," she said to his member. "We've only just begun. It's going to be a long night."

THE SHOWER WAS their next encounter. He went through the ritual he'd seen in his mind so many times—the fantasy of untying her leather sandal straps. She'd stepped out of her panties and thrown her top and bra to the side, but she still had those leather laces crisscrossing her shapely thighs and calves. Her nude little honeypot swayed from side to side as she walked towards him.

"May I untie you now?" he asked.

"I'd like that. She leaned slightly forward, hands on her lower thighs, her breasts firm and nipples knotted. He knelt before her, worshiping her body at first, looking at the smooth texture of her browned skin and the thin band of white where her incredibly small bathing suit sheltered her pussy from the sun and other prying eyes.

He touched her clit and then licked his lips.

"Just one lick. Then you untie me."

Alex's tongue slid down into her channel, the tip rimming her core and then playing round robin with her little nub. He noted her little jerking motions as he worked the little organ. He violated her rules and leaned in to put his lips on her, but she strong-armed him and held him back.

"No. You had your lick. Now untie me."

It felt like an order. He wasn't sure he was up for this, but a look down at his cock and he knew there wasn't going to be much she could say that would weaken his ardor.

After moistening his lips slowly, he said, "I like how you taste, Sydney."

"You've got a nice tongue, Alex, and you use it well. I hope you'll use it again."

"Without a doubt." He began to lean forward, but she stopped him again.

"Now you untie me," she said firmly.

Just like in his dreams, his fingers moved over the puckered flesh underneath the strapping, until he found the top ends of the sandal laces. He was careful to untie the first one, and then, just like in his dream, the upper part of his hand was dangerously close to her nude pussy again. He teased her by allowing her moist, warm lips to kiss his hand there, making him shiver and causing his cock to bounce. He began to extend his forefinger, working to impale her, but she stopped him gain.

"Untie me first, Alex."

Slowly, he untied the second knot peeling the leather strap away from her leg, kissing her inner thigh and tracing his tongue along the indentations the trusses left there.

"What do you like?" he whispered to her as he fingered her clit.

"I like that," she said in his ear.

"And this?" he asked as he slipped two fingers inside her.

"Um-hmm."

He was tasting her again.

She drew him up to a standing position, and led him to the shower. It was hard to focus, seeing the lines still embedded in her flesh as she walked. She examined him over her shoulder.

They stepped inside and she turned on the water. Taking his place behind her, he began kneading and spreading her cheeks, enjoying the luxurious feel of her flesh as he squeezed and released her butt cheeks. He inserted fingers inside her again. She hissed at his touch, the way he explored her, pinching her clit and asking her if she liked it.

She removed the oscillating spray wand from its holder, turned on the sharp, pulsing vibration and handed it to him. On his knees, he licked over her anus and then positioned the wand against her, spraying the water directly inside.

He sat on the bench. "Come here." He dropped the wand.

As she turned to face him, he hungrily searched her body before gently pulling her knees apart, inserting his thumb against her clit. Sydney squealed. His mouth was right there. He pulled on the lips of her labia with his teeth. His tongue massaged her clit. He leaned back and rubbed the water wand against her, allowing the jets to fill her while his fingers massaged her opening. He could feel Sydney sparking, readying herself to accept his cock again.

He gently turned her around and, without using his hands to guide him, slid his cock down the cleft to her vacant and wanting opening. And then he was inside her. Deep inside her.

She threw her thighs over his, straddling him, giving him deeper penetration and allowing her to move up and down on his shaft. He drew the wand around her front and pulsed against her clit again, while he pulled and pinched the little organ.

"Tell me what you like, Sydney," he whispered to her ear while he twisted her nipple.

"I like the way you are so deep, Alex."

"Yes, baby." He continued to lift his hips up, raising her feet off the shower floor, digging deeper inside her. "Like that?"

"Yes!"

The water had begun to go cold so Sydney turned it off. The remaining steam muffled her squeals as he plundered her. They adjusted. At one point, he was pressing her into the tile wall of the shower, her leg bent, and foot resting on the bench. Then she rode him from the front, her knees beside his hips on the bench seat. She pulled his hair as he felt her begin her orgasm. Her desperate moans rumbled throughout the enclosure, sending vibrations up his spine. She was losing control, urgently wrapping her legs around his waist as his pace quickened, building her climax to the brink. Her muscles clamped down on his member. His long strokes became faster and faster until he exploded, filling her.

They stared at each other without saying a word for several minutes, each exploring the other's face. Her fingers squeezed his earlobes as she bent to kiss him.

"I'm glad you stayed," she said between kisses.

"Me too. I almost didn't."

"I know." She played with the hairs that had fallen down across his brow. "Should we try the bed next?" she asked, kissing him on each eye.

"I think I'm up for that."

SHE FELT JOY emanating from the knowledge that he liked to screw with intensity. And he wouldn't be surprised, nor would he object to them going a third and perhaps a fourth round. And then they'd wait to see what the morning would bring.

She was already wishing it would never end.

CHAPTER 5

A LEX WOKE WITH a start, not sure where he had landed. He could tell bright light poured into the room, because the edges of his closed eyelids were rimmed in fire. He dared not to open them, for risk of an enormous headache, until he could adjust the shades. Experienced with Saturday morning wakeups, he waited for his head to tell him how bad the hangover was going to be before he attempted to make things worse by getting up.

But I feel fantastic!

Warmth and excited anticipation was pulsing throughout his whole body. Even his dick got hard, and then he felt her hand squeezing over it. All of a sudden, her lips were on him again, and oh boy! Was this number five? Six? Did it matter?

Alex squinted through the brightness as he adjusted his gaze. At first, the vision of Sydney straddling him, her long hair dropping to cover his thighs and her knees tightly hugging his knees, was blurry. But as she coaxed him and made loud sucking noises without trying to be delicate or ladylike, he was getting so hard and big, he felt he could screw all day.

Her head bobbed up and down on him. Her sultry eyes showed him how she liked to give orals, another very welcome surprise. He had a vague recollection of another person who liked this—oh yes, Brandy! Try as he might, he just couldn't see Brandy's face.

You're a dickhead. You can't even remember what your ex looks like?

Guilt began to rise inside his chest, like someone had stuck a rusty hook in it to fester. But then he felt those lips of Sydney's nearly sucking his cock right off the stem.

Holy Mother of God—Sorry, Joanne. He closed his eyes but still saw a faint vision of his sister, her arms crossed, a scowl on her face, white wings flaring from her upper back.

He was yanked back to the bedroom as Sydney looped her tongue around him again, sliding him deep and gently past her canines, her strong fingers squeezing his balls.

Alex lifted his head and watched her. God, she was a sight. Beautiful and strong, her tanned shoulders and upper chest bathed in morning sunlight as she worked, really worked to get him off. He so appreciated a lady with a sense of purpose, who was self-motivating. He got the sense she'd never quit.

Should I worry about this? Hell, no.

Her eyelids remained closed as she concentrated, pulling him deep inside and down her throat as her thighs powerfully pushed his legs together. Her cheeks got concave as she sucked hard. He felt her sex hungrily drill down on his left leg, rocking back and forth there, up from his knees to mid-thigh in a slow arc. When she held herself steady against him, he felt the warm wetness extracted and could feel her muscles working. He watched her ecstasy bloom over him.

For a moment all time stopped while he watched her come. Her eyebrows drew together. Her elbows pressed her tits together, showing the hardened nipples he was hungry for. But he didn't want to interrupt the perfection of her orgasm, performed like a dance, a private dance, for him and him alone.

She sat up, arching backward and moaned, clutching his legs, fucking his thigh. He reached for her clit and pressed a thumb against the little organ, and Sydney moaned again, then began to shudder. He continued to press and rub her nub back and forth. He wanted to tell her she was beautiful, that he loved watching her fly. That if he didn't come all day, he could be satisfied just watching her take her pleasure with him—any way she wanted.

His cock remained pointed to the ceiling after she removed her hands, her chest heaving for air. She had leaned back like a bow, hands bracing at his ankles. Her chest was sweaty already, her breasts like firm melons, and tiny beads of sweat formed on her upper lip. The vision of her letting the orgasm wash over her was the perfect way to start a new day.

Then she rounded her shoulders, drawing her elbows forward to squeeze her tits together, making them double in size. She lay her hands over those beautiful orbs, eyes barely open. She tweaked her nipples as she groaned again, watching him observe her pleasure.

He couldn't stay a bystander for much longer. His cock was anticipating an out-of-this-world encounter, and damn, he was going to feed it that. He needed to be inside her and feel the power of her pleasure.

He quickly drew to his knees. She allowed her body to fall back, knees bent, legs spread, ready for him. Her eyes flew open and a warm, light pink smile appeared on her full lips as the head of his cock entered her.

"Baby, I want to watch, but I need to feel it too," he said as he plunged in.

"Yes," she whispered. She threw her head back and drew him inside with her muscles.

She was slick and her lips were swollen. The wince at her right eye told him she was experiencing a little pain from their numerous lovemakings, but she bore it with pride. He didn't want to hurt her, so he asked, "You okay, sweetheart? I mean—"

She threaded her fingers through the back of his hair and pulled him to her, nibbling on his lips, "Don't say that. There isn't any part of this I don't love. I'm not a china doll."

He lost himself inside her mouth, inside her channel. He swam through all the sensations of her touch, her taste and the heady smell of their combined bodies. Each thrust made him need her more. She was no china doll. And he was so glad, he could hardly keep his heart from exploding.

She was just like him.

ALEX WAS LETTING the day fill up with sex, and he didn't feel a bit guilty. Sydney's sleeping form was draped across his chest. He was proud he'd worn her out and didn't have to be careful around her or worry about her being fragile. But his chest swelled with the full realization and pride that he'd fucked her hard, and she loved it and wanted more, but in the end, she'd collapsed. All his worries about her fled. As long as she stayed in his bed, in his arms, she would be safe. She didn't need protection. She needed a man to rock her world 24/7. She needed it like the air they breathed.

He was the same way.

With other women, Alex always felt he had to hold back. Now he'd found someone who loved intensity in life as much as he did. She was more than rare. She was the one in a billion woman he could be with for more than a few weeks of fun. He gladly accepted the addiction of her being.

Her skin was tanned, with sexy tan lines showing a thin patch of white skin on her incredible ass. Her legs went on to forever. Her thighs were more developed than most guys he knew. And man, did she know how to use them! In bed, he didn't notice their difference in height. He would get used to seeing them side-by-side, her at least four inches taller. His private Amazon. Unleashing all that intensity on him and, hopefully, him alone. He'd gladly take whatever it was she wanted to dish out.

The walls of her bedroom were light pink, which seemed odd to Alex as he didn't think of Sydney as a girl with pink things but a woman in full dress camo, or scuba gear and rebreathers. He wanted to show her how to jump out of airplanes and fire weapons. He'd never felt that way before. There was always part of himself, as a SEAL, he wanted to keep stored safely inside. But now, after this brief encounter, he suddenly wanted to share with her everything about his lifestyle.

A glass bookshelf was overflowing with trophies. Posters signed by male and female volleyball players were hung in frames on every available wall space. Some of the faces he recognized. He noticed a fitness magazine with Sydney on the cover, her arm arched back, ready to take a swing. Her ribcage showed, her back in a perfect bow shape, and her feet some four feet off the sand. The red and white volleyball floating in the air slightly above her eye level was the defenseless target of her aim. He marveled at the power of her physique.

He saw several medals hung on red, white and blue ribbons, and a team photo with the ladies holding flowers on a beach somewhere in Hawaii. She had framed the cover of an Italian magazine featuring her in her signature skimpy bathing suit, riding a scooter, her long hair flowing out under her bright red helmet.

He noticed she'd traveled all over the world, as pictures at the Great Wall of China and the Kremlin in Moscow attested. It was obvious to him that she wasn't just a beach volleyball player, but a world-class volleyball player.

It was a shame, really, that he would be leaving tomorrow for Sonoma County. He'd have to tell her soon. Over food. When they got around to eating, that is.

All the past mistakes the Team had made fixing him up with girls were forgiven. They'd found Sydney for him. Yes, they'd had a rocky start, and she definitely had some odd quirks, but then, so did he. Jumping out of helicopters at midnight with a hundred pounds on your back, into enemy territory where they burned people alive just for the fun of it, wasn't exactly normal either.

No, he would forever be grateful he'd finally found a woman just like him.

CHAPTER 6

S YDNEY WAS ANNOYED when Alex told her he was hungry. Like food was as important as sex.

Guys think like that? Thought it was the other way around.

For her, it sure was. But she humored him when he allowed her to pick the menu.

"Oysters. You need some oysters, Alex."

He looked surprised, and then he blushed. Water sluiced over his massive shoulders as he ducked under the spray and rinsed shampoo from his scalp. Man, what she could do with shoulders like that. She could spike a volleyball all the way to China if she had arms and shoulders like that.

She rubbed her thigh along the outside of his, pressing her mound into his right butt cheek. His shoulders shook slightly, and she could see he was laughing to himself.

"No," she said.

He turned around to face her, his brows coming together, a question on his lips as the glistening water dripped down his face. "Excuse me?"

"The answer is no. You were going to ask me if I ever stop needing sex."

She stood perfectly still and didn't smile, but looked deep into his eyes as if she could soak up all the deep blue she saw there. She knew she was a lethal form of something and that he had no idea what he was getting into. She hoped the excitement she saw in his return gaze held just a little fear.

A little fear is good. I'll take some of your fear, Alex. I might even be able to take a lot of it.

His eyelashes briefly dropped as he perused her body, his back to the shower head. She knew he was studying her, making a plan. Making his mind up about something. Soon he sported a wicked smile.

"What am I going to do with you, Sydney?" he whispered, stepping to her and pressing his erection between her legs. She was going to wrap her fingers around him but he pushed them away.

His right hand slid along her slit as his shaft rooted to find her throbbing honeypot. All of a sudden, he turned her around, bent her over and spread her cheeks. His cock was inside her to the hilt with one forceful thrust. Sydney saw stars. She felt like she wanted to bite the tiles off the shower walls.

SHE HAD NEVER been to the seafood grill down at the inlet. It was filled with junked boats of various sizes and in various states of repair. The small fishermen's village was more populated with dogs than fish this time of day. The grill served breakfast all day and was a favorite Team hangout after Friday night dates, he told her.

"Especially those that didn't go so well. It has some of the freshest fish in town, as well as a steady supply of oysters from all over the US."

"Perfect choice. I like it," she said.

She loved the feel of her swollen sex as Alex led her across the tiled floor. Small, rustic wooden tables were set out on the balcony. Inside, the oilcloth tables were nearly half filled. The smell was salty and aromatic in a wild sense. Sea birds hovered over piles of overturned crab pots and netting, looking for a morsel.

There were chalkboards over the bar, listing all the varieties of oysters, eggs, and beer and their prices.

Alex let out a faint groan as she leaned her back against him when they studied the menu. He drew his arms around her waist and held her tight.

"You can have all the oysters you need, my dear." His whisper was raspy. He followed it up with a tiny bite to her earlobe. Sydney's chest began to pound and her ears buzzed.

"What do you recommend?" she asked.

"I like Hog Island. Drake's Bay are good. The barbequed ones are stellar, and so are the garlic pesto."

She hadn't known there were so many varieties. She turned to the side in his arms, careful to let her left breast press against his. "Aren't the raw ones best for you?"

He was smiling, getting ready to say something when a heavyset cook in a white apron slapped him on the back.

"How the hell are you, Alex? Haven't seen you since the—"

The cook had clearly started saying something that shouldn't be repeated in mixed company and abruptly stopped.

"Since my freedom party? That's okay, Griff." He stepped back and gave Sydney a tiny push at the sides of her hips, placing her between him and the cook. "Griff, this is Sydney. Sydney, meet Griff."

She extended her hand and felt the swollen callused paw of a man who worked hard. "Nice to meet you, Griff." Her squeeze was returned in kind.

Griff gave Alex a wink. "You guys know what you want?"

Sydney was suddenly starved. "Yes. I want blueberry pancakes, double the butter and syrup, a dozen of the barbeque oysters, and a dozen Hog Island raw with salsa." She turned to see Alex's surprised smile. She decided to push the envelope a bit more. "What are you having?" she asked him.

He stepped back. "Whoa. You really going to eat all that?"

"Yes. Why, you don't think I can?"

"I know better than to challenge you on that." He nodded toward Griff. "While she's protecting her pancakes from my fork, I'll have a seafood scramble." He checked her face and added, "I'll take a dozen of your garlic pesto."

He led them outside to the balcony overlooking the inlet. The crisp breeze tickled her cheeks. It was the right kind of invigorating. A light gray fog hovered over the cove.

Griff served them each fresh squeezed orange juice. "On the house," he said as he turned to the kitchen. Stopping, he asked, "Coffee?"

"Sure," Alex answered. "That okay?" he asked her. "I mean, it's a little caffeine. No chocolate in our menu this morning."

"Not for me, thanks," she said to Griff, who went in search of Alex's coffee.

She loved that he'd remembered and was trying to calibrate something. "Meaning, is it safe?"

He grabbed her hand and kissed her palm. "Just checking your temperature, sweetheart."

"Since you asked, I do have to watch caffeine and

chocolate, especially together. I work out hard too. Occasionally, I can ease up on one of the three. As far as zombie movies? I have no clue. And I don't even want to find out, either."

He laughed. "So we just happened to hit the perfect trifecta last night."

"Yes, in more ways than one, sailor."

Alex began to blush, which was a huge surprise. He continued to hold her hand as he lay it back down on the table. She wondered if there was something on his mind he was struggling with. His face dropped the smile as he looked up. "I'm going on a little trip up to Sonoma County tomorrow and I'll be gone a couple of weeks, I think."

She sighed. Of all the bad luck. Maybe this would be good. She could focus on traveling to some venues to check out other players in her partner search. She didn't have a tournament for a month. Perhaps this time she'd really train the way she knew she was supposed to. Unless he was asking her to go with him.

"I'm going with several of the other guys, and we're staying with friends, or I'd ask you to go along."

She liked that he'd asked, at least. "Thank you. I have to get prepared for a tournament next month, and I'm still scouting the talent down here."

He nodded.

"Do they even have beaches in Sonoma County?"

"Not like these." He put his elbows on the table and leaned in, taking her hand in his again and kissing it. "But they do have oysters." He followed up his kiss with a wink.

"That's useful information. I'll have to file that away for future reference."

The food arrived. Sydney lathered her pancakes with butter and syrup, but before she could take a bite Alex scored a large slice and had it in his mouth.

"You were right about that. I do have to protect my pancakes, don't I?"

"Yup." His smile was deliciously covered in butter and syrup.

They ate in silence. Since there was a time limit to their encounter now, Sydney wanted some answers.

"So tell me about yourself, Alex. You ever been married?"

"How do you know I'm not married now?"

"Because I think you wouldn't do that. I'm rarely wrong. A married man has a different way about him. They make you walk through the back door. They have secrets, big ones. I don't get that with you. Am I wrong?"

"Nope, sweetheart. I'm divorced. And yes, this was the scene of my freedom party a few months ago." He sipped his coffee. "I live in an apartment with three other bachelors. But I was married, for about three months." He wiggled his eyebrows up and down, checking her reaction.

Sydney's radar was piqued. "Impossible to know everything about someone in a month."

Alex shrugged and examined his empty plate, and then noticed hers was nearly empty too. "We did good work here. Mission accomplished. Now I won't be able to move all day."

"That's too bad." She allowed her lip to droop. "So you were telling me why you were married for a month. Why bother?"

"It was sort of dumb. You'll probably not think very highly of me. Ryan and I—Ryan's my roommate—we went to Vegas with our girlfriends. It was just a lark. Her name is Brandy—my ex."

"I'll bet you didn't know much about her either."

"No. We don't talk that much. She's kind of a dancer."

"Ah." Sydney was having too much fun dragging the details out of Alex. But she did notice he didn't describe her in the past tense.

"We took them up to Vegas, and we had a fun weekend. A little over the top We got a little smashed. It seemed like a good idea at the time." He stopped, inhaled and then continued. "Well, we did a double wedding at the Elvis Chapel."

"I hear that happens a lot up there. I had a friend

who married a guy from Spain when we were over there playing. Had a terrible time getting it annulled. Alcohol was involved in that one, too."

"No, she knew. I mean, it wasn't that serious. I should have never done it. We laugh about it now."

There was that present tense again. "That how you look at marriage?" She needed to watch his reaction. He was being tested again, and yes, the return glance he gave her indicated he fully understood.

"Of course not, Sydney." He released her hand and sat back. "When I find the right girl, it won't be like that at all."

"So you still see her or are you fully single?"

"That's a lot of questions so early on a Saturday morning."

"If you can't handle it, I'll stop." She saw him flinch. She needed to turn on the syrup a little more. Her direct approach was beginning to scare him. On the other hand, it was important to know whether seeing him was a waste of time. She didn't like to waste time.

"Why don't we reverse this for a few minutes while I finish my coffee. And then I'll have to be moving on, okay? Gotta get ready for my trip."

She hesitated. He was good at brushing people off. Regardless of their world-class evening and morning, he could separate that. He could walk away. Her heart fluttered slightly as she realized perhaps she could not. Or just didn't want to.

"So what do you want to know?"

"Who are you, Sydney?"

And boy was that the right question! Not who are you dating, who do you hang around, what do you do all day? This was usually the question that came up after the second or third date, just before she was about to exit stage right.

Her answer was measured and well-practiced.

"I want more out of life than life's given me so far, but I'm not complaining. I just want more of it. I want the *juice* of life, not to *live* life. I'm looking to get a good partner and travel the world playing volleyball until my knees ache and my back or shoulder gives out. And after volleyball? Who knows what I'll be able to do at eighty?" She gave him the smile she'd given so many other dumbstruck men over the few years since she'd been dating. It was always the same. It also usually got the same reaction.

But this time, she saw something ignite inside Alex. The backdrop of lonely sea gull cries, the salty gentle breeze and sounds of metal clanging as work began late at the docks, only enhanced the excitement brewing in her belly. She was struck with the beauty and power of something maybe dangerous about this man. And also something so beautiful her eyes watered.

CHAPTER 7

T HE GOOD-BYE WITH Sydney had been slow and sensual. She nearly got him naked again. He was trying to act casual, but the parting irritated him. They exchanged phone numbers so they could stay in touch at least by text. He normally didn't do this, but today it had been his idea.

On the drive up to his apartment he couldn't help but chuckle. Yes, he was satisfied in several departments, but just when he'd finally met a woman he could spend the whole weekend with, he had made other plans.

He thought about their parting. His mood suddenly soured. He had turned, gotten in his Hummer and never looked back. That wasn't how he wanted to leave it, but what the hell was he supposed to do?

He pushed those thoughts aside and took a deep breath, donning the psychological clothes he needed for his brotherhood encounter. It was time to get the guys, get his gear and get out of town. End of story. That's all there was to it.

Nick, the former member of SEAL Team 3, had just medically retired and was now full time at the winery in Sonoma County. Several other guys who had put their ten years in and were suffering from some tough injuries were looking into getting into the wine business as well. Although Alex was completely short on funds, as were a couple of the other men, he seemed to be the glue that held everyone together. Besides, he'd promised Zak's new bride he'd keep an eye on the one-eyed SEAL. Both Zak and Amy were from Sonoma County so a move and change of career might be a good fit.

Coop was waiting for him at the apartment.

"You're late."

"But I'm fed and showered. Just got to get my duty bag."

Coop followed him up the stairs, passing the elevator they never took. "Kyle's not coming, kid." The tall medic always addressed him that way, and it had nothing to do with age. Coop would be going on his eighth deployment with SEAL Team 3, having served on an East Coast Team for his first tour. Alex only had three tours and five years to his name, so he was senior to all the froglets, but junior in rank to Coop. Kyle was their platoon leader.

"What's up with that?" Alex opened the front door. The apartment smelled awful. A young woman in a skimpy silk teddy ran around the corner from the kitchen, waving at Zak as she dove into Cory's bedroom and slammed the door without saying a word.

"Remember those days, Coop?"

"I do, I do indeed. Although they never got too far in my Babemobile. And slamming doors was not in the program, mostly because those doors don't slam."

"I've heard stories about that thing. You still have it?"

"Oh, I let one of the froglets borrow it for a couple of months—he's got it back at the beach, waiting for his housing allowance to kick in. Libby says it's an eyesore, and she makes me park it down the street at a gas station when it's home."

"Can you blame her, Coop?" Alex noticed that Cory's friend had made coffee. Although early afternoon, Alex was happy for the steaming cup. He poured another one with lots of cream.

"You want one?"

Coop scrunched up his nose. "Nah."

"Okay, well, I'm taking this in to Cory. Maybe this will help him get up."

Coop shrugged and walked to the glass sliders leading to their balcony as Alex approached the closed bedroom door. He banged on it with his fist, being careful not to damage the hollow core surface. "Hey Cory, you in a gentlemanly pose so I can bring you some coffee?" Alex cocked his head and leaned his ear against the pressboard door. He could hear whispering and the tussle of sheets.

Cory's normally neat appearance was completely obliterated by the dirty-looking stubble and tufted light brown hair resembling the corn stalk scalp on a rag doll.

"Thanks, man," Cory said as he reached for the mug.

"Coop's here. Everyone's gonna be arriving in like ten minutes. Where's Ryan and Jake?"

"They're with Lucas and Zak, picking up supplies. Don't worry, they'll not want to hold up Kyle."

"Not Kyle you have to worry about. Coop's in charge."

"Kyle's not coming?"

"Coop says no." Alex heard the shower going off in the background. "You think you can wrap things up and get your butt out here?"

"What's got you all hot and bothered? Didn't it work out last night with the volleyball chick?" Cory sipped his coffee.

Alex wanted to punch him, but he quickly reeled it in. The irritation surprised him. He tried not to say anything, but he could see Cory was going to poke him with that big fat needle until he spilled. "She's fine."

Cory grinned from ear to ear. "Sweet."

"Yes, asshole. You guys are off the hook for awhile."

"Even better. Well, Alex, you see, miracles happen every day. So if it can happen to you, it can happen to me. Not that I'm looking, of course."

"Of course not. You're just sampling the merchandise."

Cory cleared his throat as the lady behind him walked past the crack in the door without a stitch of clothing on. Cory managed to roll his eyes, balancing his hot coffee mug, stepped outside the doorway and closed the door behind him. "Kinda glad no one came home last night, if you know what I mean."

Coop approached the bedroom. "What the fuck you doin' Cory? Get your butt out here. The guys pulled up downstairs so you're the last one to get ready."

"Yeah, not cool, man. You live here," added Alex.

Cory held up two fingers and quickly retreated behind the closed door.

"Honestly," Coop said as he stepped back, "you bachelor guys got no responsibilities. You'd think you could be on time for once. Heck, I had to clean up dishes, fold my own clothes, change a very nasty diaper and mow the lawn before Libby would let me out of the house, and I'm the first to be ready here.

"Coop, don't see how you do it."

"Well there's a little secret to that," Coop said, following Alex into his bedroom. While Alex pulled out a large duty bag, stuffing it with clothing and his medic's kit as well as his personal items, Coop continued. "I make sure it's worth it to her. That's the secret. It's so fuckin' simple. I don't know why guys can't figure that out."

Alex partially zipped up the bag, and after almost forgetting, pulled a toothbrush and a couple other small items from the medicine cabinet and threw them inside. "Happy wife, happy life, right?"

"That's it."

Pounding on the apartment door followed. It had enough force to rattle the windows. Cory beat them to the door and let Zak, Lucas, Jake, Ryan, Mark and Luke burst in, carrying grocery bags and ice chests. Mark had four bags of chipped ice balanced on his shoulders.

"Where's Kyle?" asked Lucas. Zak stood behind his friend, rubbing underneath his eyepatch with his forefinger.

"He's got some event Collins wants him to attend. He'll follow us in a couple of days," Coop informed them.

"We going early on our next vacation?" Ryan asked.

They used the term vacation whenever they were not sure about their security. No one took this lightly. Last week, someone on one of the other Teams had discovered one of the SEALs' apartments had been bugged.

"Nope. He didn't say that," Coop informed them.

For the next five minutes, the team worked silently, packing the chests, organizing it so nearly every square inch was filled. They added the ice last. Cory's date made a quick exit and the team followed her down the hallway, but avoided the elevator she took. They loaded the gear in three separate vehicles as she peeled off and drove away.

This was to be a road trip, of course, but it still was a mission of sorts. That meant that talk was minimal. If there was pressure, there'd be the classic smack talk and some mild jokes being pulled. But today, the muted caravan of two Hummers and one four-door, long-bed pickup headed off the island and toward the freeway north.

ROUGHLY SEVEN HOURS later, they arrived at Nick and Devon's winery, *Sophie's Choice*, in Santa Rosa. Alex was driving the bachelor contingent, Coop had Zak and Lucas, and Mark came with Luke. Alex had only been up one time before. He whistled. "Wow. This is spectacular!"

Though it was night, the buildings and driveway were lit up and it appeared there was some kind of reception going on. A catering truck was parked along the left side of the tasting room.

Their headlights flashed on green vines and well-tended rows bursting with tiny green fruit. Alex rolled down his window and inhaled the crisp night air. Colorful gardens were illuminated around the brand new tasting room entrance. The building's copper roof spires extended into the sky, above the guests on the balconies overlooking the vineyards and valley below. There was music coming from the downstairs level, carrying across the valley floor.

"Lookin' good. So I guess the winery business is booming," said Jake.

Nick met Mark's truck, which had been first in the driveway. He directed them all to drive around the back. The parking lot to the tasting room was filled with several black and white limos as well as a dozen or more expensive cars.

"Damn! I didn't come dressed for this party. You know about this, Alex?" asked Cory.

"Nope. Mark made all the arrangements."

Alex parked next to Coop's Hummer, and they began exiting the vehicles. He recognized Devon, wearing a shepherd's white top over a gathered skirt. She wore red, flowered gardening boots and had flowers pinned to her hair. The white top accentuated the huge bulge in her belly.

"Mamacita! Look at you!" Mark said as he ran to her and gently picked her up in his arms. Devon was giggling. "No briefcase, no suit, no high heels. Wow. You look fantastic," he said as he put her down.

Devon appeared to glow in the evening light. Alex could see she was embarrassed.

"Guys!" Mark said enthusiastically. "This is Devon, Nick's Devon, the lady of the house." He turned back to her. "You shouldn't have thrown a party for us. That was really nice of you!"

She grinned. "No, this was very last minute. We book up fast, but we had a cancellation. It's a private wedding, a fellow vet. But from some of the ladies I've met tonight, I don't think they'd mind if you crashed the party. I'll have to ask the bride and groom. Wasn't sure you guys would be up for anything like that with the long drive."

"Seriously, Devon," began Ryan, "I think with a shower we'd be ready for anything. But I didn't exactly bring dress clothes."

"I think they might like you just in blue jeans. I was going to gift you the lavender winery T-shirts so you wouldn't be expected to dress up. You could go as part of the staff—and yes, sorry, but they're lavender! If you want them, they're yours."

"Yes, ma'am," came the uniform response.

Jake scrunched up his nose and whispered to Alex, "Lavender? We gotta wear lavender?"

Alex stepped on his foot to shut him up.

Nick took his place beside his wife, placing an arm around her waist. "Come, and I'll show you guys where you're staying. Leave your gear. We can unload all that in a bit.

The group followed behind Nick, who was punching and chatting with Mark. Alex knew the two of them had been close, and Mark had at one time been a special friend to Nick's dying sister, Sophie.

Nick addressed his audience just as a scream and then clapping went up inside the venue hall. "I'm guessing someone might have been showing off in there. Either that or the cake fell over."

Alex liked it here. The evening was warm and filled with excitement.

"We have a nice guest house, behind our place. It's got beds, if some of you don't mind bunks. We get a lot of families staying here, especially during crush. Ecotourism is a new thing here in Sonoma County."

He led the way around the side of their modern two story home made from recycled material, to the bunkhouse behind. He stepped up on the wooden porch, lined with five rocking chairs. In front of the porch was built a stone fire pit encircled with log stools. Nick propped the door open. "Welcome to Sophie's Choice."

Everyone piled inside. The space was rustic, but had an efficiency kitchen and a large community table. The fireplace was already roaring.

"Bedroom is through that doorway, and it's set up to sleep eight," Nick shouted. Jake headed for it. "Only one shower, I'm sorry to say. We got an instant hot water heater, but if you guys aren't careful, some of you will still have to take a cold one." As an afterthought he added, "Unless some of you want to shower together."

He got a pillow tossed at him for his efforts.

MARK BROUGHT HIS stuff into Nick and Devon's house, since they had a room set up for him in there. Coop walked up behind Alex saying, "You knew about Mark and Sophie?"

"His wife?"

"No, his wife is Sophia. Met her after Sophie, that's Nick's sister, passed on. I know Mark's a little emotional about coming back here, but he's fine. Good that they're taking him in the house. Probably have a lot to catch up on." Coop slapped Alex on the shoulder. "Can you give me a hand with one of these ice chests?"

In a half hour everything was stowed, beds selected, showers completed. Their favorite workout music was booming in the great room, choruses of angels and titles like "One Against The Thousand." It was battle music they also listened to when they were heading out to a halo drop. It drowned out the music in the hall. The group, all in lavender T-shirts except for Jake, took stock of themselves before heading over to the party.

"I'm going to post naked pictures on FB of anyone who takes a shot of us in lavender," Zak said.

"As a matter of fact, gents, leave your cell phones behind so you won't be tempted to do something really stupid," Coop demanded. "That's not optional. It's an order."

That was never a guarantee, but Alex was glad he requested it. Ladies and alcohol and being away from home made for one dangerous combination.

Just before he lay his phone down, he noticed he'd gotten a text from Sydney.

Did you arrive safe and sound?

He answered back, *yes, ma'am.* Then he turned his phone off and left with the group.

CHAPTER 8

SYDNEY WAS GOING to run over to one of the local beaches to check out a tournament that was nearing a close when she got a call from her girlfriend, Carly.

"Hey, Syd. I've been thinking about your offer. Maybe we can have a shot."

"Seriously?" Sydney was elated. Carly had been a competitor in college, but they'd become close friends. They'd played together in a couple of side tournaments before Leah was free, and they worked well together. "Let's try it."

"You haven't found anyone yet?"

"No, and Leah's looking doubtful. I hired Jack to help me train. We're scheduled to do a mixed tournament next month. I haven't done one in nearly a month."

"Ouch. Sounds like me. We'll have some work to do, then. So, when I get back to San Diego later in the week, let's talk."

"Where are you?"

"I'm living with my old my roommate, you remember Jenn?"

"I do. The soccer player?"

"That's Jenn. Got herself coaching junior high girls here. I came up for a little R & R, and, well, I got hooked on the area and started coaching high school girls and now some Club ball. I thought about your offer, and I think I'd like to try it. I think it might work, but we need to talk first."

Sydney couldn't believe her luck. "Of course. That's way cool. When will you be back?"

"A couple of days, maybe longer, but I think I'll head down Thursday at the latest. Can you wait that long for our sit-down?"

"Shoot, I've been looking for three months now. You were my first choice, Carly." On a whim, she asked, "Where do you live now?"

"Little town up here called Healdsburg. Sonoma County."

Sydney's pulse quickened. "Is that near Santa Rosa?"

"Yup. Just a couple of towns up the freeway from there. I train in Santa Rosa."

"Want some company? Or, would I be intruding?"

"You? Come up here? You're kidding, of course."

"No." She tried to tone down her eagerness.

Breathe! Are you completely nuts, Sydney? Think about this!

"I think Jenn would be cool with it."

"I'll stay at a motel. No worries."

"God, Sydney, you seriously want to come all the way up here?"

"Why not?" Of course she had some nagging doubts about what Alex would think. And how the heck would she even find him? It would be a needle in a haystack unless she called him.

After another shower, her second after her first steamy one with Alex that morning, she examined the tousled sheets on her bed. She dropped her towel and stood naked in the afternoon sunlight, staring down at the evidence of their exciting romp together.

There hadn't been enough talk, she noted. Probably too much sex, although he didn't seem to mind that her need had been off the charts last night and this morning.

I'll blame it on the Junior Mints and the caffeine.

She sat, spreading her hand over the comforter, smoothing the lines and wrinkles, then pulling it up tight. She picked up the pillows, put them both to her face one at a time and inhaled his scent, getting lost in the sensory memory of how his body felt next to hers. After the fluffing was completed, she replaced them in their respective slots.

Did men know they left a scent? It was as distinctive as perfume on a different woman or cologne on a man. She knew it was biology. Somewhere inside her sensitive body was a delicate scale that measured and weighed everything. Along with the taste of his mouth, the feel of his touch and the sound of his breathing, his manly scent was part of what she would miss. And now craved.

Stop it, Sydney. This isn't you. But unlike other times, she just couldn't get Alex out of her mind. Though the encounter had been intense, it was still way too short.

This wasn't fair. She doubted men had the same bodily mechanism as women did. She'd heard someone give a lecture in college about how natural selection gave off the pheromones that in ancient times told a woman the man she was attracted to would pleasure her greatly and give her healthy children. This would happen long before the first kiss, but was *sealed* with the taste of him on her tongue. Was it something every woman thought about like she did? That first kiss was the clincher. "The taste of *the other*," her professor had said, "becomes the total object of the female's desire. When he is no longer *the other* but recognized as home and hearth and part of the woman's protection, they are truly joined as one. It's not sex. It's biology. The will to build the species."

It was a concept she believed in, though had never experienced herself until now. Most of her life, in relation to men, she was busy making sure she was in control, making sure she was protected in case they let her down. Making sure she would not only survive, but come out on top. She was into taking chances, but not if the price was too high. And after all that, she made it sport. The sport of it became the frosting on top, made it fun.

She threw on her clothes, slipping on her well-worn workout shoes last. At the bottom of the closet was her weekend bag. She stared down at it in the shadows, half covered by a long dress hanging overhead. Stooping, she picked it up, examined its empty belly, and then threw it on the bed, as if it had burned her hands.

No Sydney. This isn't wise.

Her inner mother was scolding her as she grabbed several pairs of underwear from her top dresser drawer, several T-shirts, sports bras and bras. One lacy one in black. A black nightgown she only wore in mixed company.

No. No. No.

Her toilet kit, favorite brush, two baseball caps, two pairs of sunglasses, extra suntan lotion, a pair of flats, a sweater and one dress—left on the hanger, still encased in the plastic wrap from the cleaners.

She checked her Apple Watch. It was barely two o'clock. She'd driven to San Francisco once in a hurry in less than six hours. One to two hours more and she'd be in Sonoma County. She could find a place to stay, have a good meal and plan for her meet with Carly tomorrow.

With the tournament coming up, it isn't wise. Stay home and train, her inner mother shouted.

But it isn't one of my qualifying tournaments, just something to keep in shape, something to help my mindset, which is pretty focused right now, she argued. She knew she was justifying something that made no logical sense. Because it wasn't logic. It was something else.

Your future on the pro circuit is a figment of your imagination unless you get your body in shape, Sydney.

She knew it was true, but she continued to pack anyway.

This mixed doubles tournament was with an old coach of hers who she later became involved with in college. Although competitive, the only thing Sydney had to concern herself about was him keeping his hands to himself. Even his new wedding ring seemed to make little difference to him. He was a player and was still playing, even though married. He would never change, even though he had helped her train in the past. Now, without a partner, she needed his expertise because he knew her ability better than anyone else on the circuit. He knew what a competitive machine she was, what her strengths and weaknesses were. It was worth it to put up with a little of his BS. She was focused on the game and hoped he would be as well. Maybe he'd agree to coach the both of them. Her partnering with Carly solved more than one problem.

Again, Sydney, you're justifying. You're going to have to make a stand with him.

She nodded. "Yes. I can handle him. I can handle anyone. I'll deal with it later."

She zipped her bag up, determined to go on that road trip. If she ran into Alex, would he understand or would it scare him away? She knew it was a risk.

What are you doing, Sydney? Stop. Just stop right now and think.

"I can do this. I'm focused on the goal. I just have to make sure I keep it between the lines. She was taking a risk, stepping outside her normal routine for a chance at something she'd just had a taste of. Was it wrong to go after that chance or forever regret not doing so? That was something she wasn't willing to do.

She slung her bag over her shoulder.

At the doorway, she turned and took a look at her pink trophy room, as she'd always called her bedroom. Now she saw it for what it was. It wasn't her future. It was her past.

THE TOP WAS down on her Murano, and as the sun began to sink low in the horizon, it began to get cold. Several times she'd had the same nagging doubts she was doing the right thing. She considered calling Alex several times, but restrained herself.

She turned on the heated seats as she descended into the Bay Area. Approaching and then driving through Palo Alto, she recalled competing in tournaments at San Jose State and Stanford. She'd spent time as an Olympic hopeful at a training camp there two years ago, and had earned a bid to try out for the US Women's Volleyball Team. Of course she was disappointed when she wasn't chosen even as an alternate. But now she was free to go after the lucrative sponsorships the pro Beach Volleyball circuit had to offer.

Crossing the Golden Gate bridge at sunset was a treat she hadn't expected. The red steel contrasted with the darkening blue of the sky and the gray fog beginning to roll in. Looking west, she saw the Farallon Islands.

That means luck will be on my side.

To the right, a long container ship was making its slow way out of the mouth of the bay. The little boats were returning to shore, a couple of tour boats still hovered around Alcatraz for a few more stolen minutes.

Through the Rainbow Tunnel she held her breath,

just as she had done as a little girl when her dad would drive her in his convertible to a volleyball camp somewhere up north. She'd grown up tall and very quickly. He called her his little giraffe.

She allowed herself a few tender memories of the happy days that existed before her father had taken ill.

Her phone chirped. It was Jack. She looked for evidence of a Highway Patrol, then carefully installed her earpiece and answered.

"Hi, Jack."

"You up for dinner? Thought we could make a workout plan for the next couple of weeks. I'm free. Barb's at her sister's."

"Sorry. I'm on my way to do a little scouting. I'm already in San Francisco."

"San Francisco? Who are you checking out?"

She wasn't going to tell Jack until she'd had the talk with Carly. "Actually I'm meeting an old friend from college. She knows some ladies who are looking. Haven't met them yet."

"Uh-huh. Okay, then. How long will you be gone?"

"Oh, just two maybe three days. Not long."

"Sounds like you're driving."

"Of course! Gives me time to think."

"Just wish you'd think a little more about us."

Her belly clenched. "Jack, there is no *us.*"

"Well, there sure used to be. You ever dream about

those days?"

She was about to hang up on him. "That was a long time ago and never should have happened. You were my coach."

"*Former* coach. Sydney, I'm still a good coach. You never give me a chance."

"You promised, Jack. Remember? You bring this shit up and I walk. Remember that promise you made?"

The other end of the line was silent. She didn't work to fill the air space, making it easy on him. She had to be tough with him or he'd never stop going after her.

He finally sighed. "Okay then. Let me know when you're on your way home. And be safe. I've got some big plans for the summer. You'll love them."

"Will do, Jack. Give my best to Holly." She hung up before Jack could react to the fact that she knew Holly McGiver, the six-foot-seven middle from UCLA was his current flame.

She's probably on a recruiting road trip with her team.

Even if Sydney had been interested in Jack, she wasn't going to be his or anybody's number two or three. She was only interested in being a number one.

SYDNEY ARRIVED IN Santa Rosa after it had gone dark

outside. Taking a motel downtown, she put the top back up and carried her things to the room. She had her third shower of the day and sat naked on the bed. Her hand hovered over her cell phone, as if some secret power would lift it up to her palm.

She texted Alex. *Did you arrive safe and sound?*

The answer came right back. *Yes ma'am.*

She asked him another question. *Having fun? How are your friends?*

She waited for several minutes. When the answer didn't come, she turned off her phone and tucked herself into bed. The cool, unfamiliar sheets felt soothing to her skin as she made a mental list of all the things she'd need to do tomorrow.

Would it be fortunate or unfortunate to run into Alex? Would he be happy to see her? Then the import of her decision hit her.

What if Alex was up here to meet someone *else*? Could there be another lady in his life?

CHAPTER 9

THE PARTY WAS in full swing when the SEALs entered the reception. They were spotted immediately. Alex and several others had dance partners who'd had a lot to drink. Coop declined all invitations, as did Zak and Lucas, but the bachelors were in clover. Mark found Nick. He and Luke stood in the corner laughing at the spectacle of members of SEAL Team 3 in lavender shirts, while Coop, Zak, and Lucas hit the chow line.

Alex became extremely self-conscious when someone began taking pictures. He hoped it hadn't leaked out who they were and what they did for work. He looked for Devon but couldn't find her in the undulating crowd.

The next set was a slow dance, and he found himself holding up a pretty blonde in a bridesmaid's dress. She peered up at him dreamily.

"You a friend of Brandy or Josh?"

He could tell she was having difficulty talking. Her balance was off as well, and soon her chest pushed into his. She hung onto his shoulders and then slipped one arm down around his waist. Alex could hardly move. He was literally dragging her across the dance floor.

"I think you need to have a seat, Missy."

"Oh, such a gentleman!" She giggled in his arms and lost her balance again.

"Let me help you. I think you've had a little too much champagne."

"Yup. Guilty." She winked at him, but her other eye didn't focus at all. "You've heard the story, ever a bridesmaid, never a bride. That's me."

He thought perhaps she'd start to cry on him. He searched for a chair nearby before she started to resist him.

"No. I wanna dance." She tried, and this time was successful at righting herself before she pressed her body tightly against his. "I got myself a handsome young stud. I intend to take full advantage of it. Make all my pretty girlfriends jealous." She gave him a sheepish grin. Alex chuckled.

"You're pretty."

"You think so?" She still had a tinge of Texas in her accent, but it had been stomped out by years of living in California. She batted her eyelashes at him, raised one eyebrow, and licked her lips. Without warning, she leaned backward and Alex had to bend quickly to catch her before she hit the floor. He righted her, with effort, and was grateful he hadn't strained his back. Several of the other ladies on the dance floor squealed and came over. Alex felt like a tree covered in butterflies.

"Again," said one ginger-haired little thing.

"Yes! We want to see it again," said another.

Alex's dance partner gave him a wicked stare, albeit still not focusing or making eye contact. "He's all mine," she said and then collapsed against his chest again. "Hands off. You're too late." She regained her balance and twirled in his arms, winding up with her back and considerably sized rear pressing against his groin. But it was the position of his hands that drew the attention from the crowd. Both palms were on her breasts. "He's mine, girls!" She threw her arms in the air so they could see her total surrender. Alex quickly adjusted his grip on the drunk blonde, while still propping her up. Their audience melted into the crowd, but the whole room was looking at him in his lavender T-shirt.

Alex scoured the room for one of his team buds and at last found Jake, who immediately understood the situation and sprang into action.

"So, do you think I'm sexy, Mr. Body Builder? God, would you look at those arms? You lift weights for a living?" She'd gripped his biceps, stubbornly not moving her feet.

Alex used what little balance he had left to lift her off the ground and deposit her in a chair. When Jake arrived to assist him, the girl looked between the two of them.

"I think I've died and gone to Heaven." She blinked several times, waiting for a response.

Just in time, Nick arrived. "I've got it, boys. Sorry about that," he whispered under his breath.

"You want me to get Devon, or someone?" Alex asked.

"Go get the bride, if you can find her. You're one of the bridesmaids, aren't you, sweetheart?" he said to the girl.

The blonde was enjoying the sight of now three handsome men in front of her.

"Lordy, I just cannot believe my luck." She fluffed her hair up and began to focus on Nick.

Alex tore through the dance floor, scoured the sides for something white, looking for the bride. He felt the tap on his shoulder and heard a familiar voice.

"Hey Alex."

Pivoting slowly, he came face to face with his ex-wife, Brandy. She was dressed in all white: the bride. When the bridesmaid asked him who he was friends with, it never occurred to him it would be *his* Brandy.

"Oh wow." He cursed himself, but he couldn't

think of anything else to say. "Brandy. I didn't know—"

"Of course not. How could you?" She delivered him a nasty, hurt look he felt he deserved fully. "You never returned any of my calls."

"I'm sorry, Brandy. Weren't we on deployment?" She quickly shook her head and put her hands on her hips. He drew his hand up to the backside of his neck. He honestly didn't remember getting any calls from her. Not that he would have returned them. He sucked it in and decided to just apologize. "I'm sorry, sweetheart. I really am."

"Ahh. Such a heartbreaker. I wish I could believe you. And now you've come to gloat. Ruin my wedding, is that right?"

"No. Absolutely not. That's unfair."

"When Devon told me some friends of Nick's were here, and asked my permission, I thought to myself, *What are the odds?* Well, no matter. That's all history now." She turned in front of him. "How do I look?"

"You look gorgeous, Brandy. I really mean that."

"Sure."

"No, I'm serious. I've never seen you—"

The music had stopped between songs. Alex heard his name shouted above the crowd.

"Alex!"

He'd forgotten about Nick.

"Brandy, one of your bridesmaids is really, really

drunk, and—"

"The one you were feeling up? Her name's Daphne."

"No, Brandy, she's drunk. She's out of her mind. Please, can you help us out?"

"Honestly," she said as she gripped her gown and kept pace with him across the dance floor. "You would think a bunch of SEALs would know how to handle this."

Daphne was passed out in Nick's arms, who had shielded her from falling over backward in the chair. Alex couldn't find Jake anywhere.

"Let's get her over to the couch. You take her feet," commanded Nick. While they were moving her, Nick raised his head. "I see you guys know each other?"

"She's my ex," Alex whispered.

"Oops. Sucks to be you, then."

They placed a pillow under her head as Daphne regained consciousness. Several of the other ladies moved in around them and took over, bringing water and a cool damp towel.

Coop presented himself. "I should take a look, Nick," the tall medic said.

"No. Don't want you involved Coop. We have to call the paramedics. Those are the rules. Don't want you involved."

Coop still watched to make sure no one was doing

anything that would further aggravate Daphne's condition. She was soon able to sit up and drink a little water, and then devoured a finger sandwich. The music began again and the crowd turned back to their partying.

Brandy grabbed Alex's arm. "Come on, Alex. One time for old time's sake?"

"Well, I'm not quite sure this is proper. I mean—"

"Oh come on. I finally get to wear a gorgeous white gown, have my wedding in a beautiful place, officiated by a minister who doesn't wear sequins. Humor me, Alex. Give me the sendoff I deserve."

She had a point. "What about your husband?"

She perused the room. "Well, he's not here to object. Besides, he knows you."

"Say what?"

"Dance with me, and I'll tell you."

The song was a little too fast for a slow dance, which was a relief to Alex, who didn't want to be touching Brandy right now. He'd already managed to get his share of scowls.

But she was the bride after all. So the deejay changed it up to a slow song. She gave Alex a sweet smile, with those pink, pouty lips he tried not to stare at.

Damn.

It was hard to pretend not to have any connection with Brandy. And he did feel bad about what had happened. He never should have married her in the first place. They'd used each other all they could, and then it was over quick. She was uncomplicated and just lovely. But not really the type of woman he needed.

"Josh is a SWCC Team guy," Brandy said, throwing her head back and raising her eyebrows.

He was impressed. "You said he knows me?"

"Not really." She was wicked beautiful, but very dangerous. "He used to come in almost as often as you did, toward the end." She swung her chin up, her little sparkling crystal earrings dangling, catching light from all around the room.

"I see. Did you—?" What the hell was he doing? What difference did it make?

"There was a time when he was leaving and you were coming back. But just a little." Her smile was shy.

"When we were married?"

"Only once."

Shit. This was turning out to be such a bad idea, getting worse by the minute. As he tried to move over the dance floor, his legs felt like glass. He wanted to throw Brandy over his knee and give her a good spank, and he had absolutely no right to do so. But he was coming off the rails. His control was slipping and the awareness of this only made it worse.

He needed to do a jump, or go swim in the ocean, or run ten miles. It was all feeling too civil for him. And here he was in a lavender fucking T-shirt. He was a trained killer, a Navy SEAL, for Chrissakes. This wasn't the life he was supposed to lead. This was the pretend cardboard life of someone else who should be standing here holding Brandy and giving her everything she wanted. He felt like an alien species.

He smiled down at her. She wasn't even trying to be present for him, but was more interested in how the crowd saw the two of them dancing. She enjoyed pressing herself into his thigh, but not so obvious that the crowd or her husband would see. He wished she wouldn't do that. He wanted to be anywhere else but here.

Alex remembered what he'd been doing just this morning. He wished Sydney was up here. He'd take her skydiving when they got finished at the winery. Maybe he'd take her to the shooting range.

But of course that was a stupid thought. Right now, he was locked in a tense drama for the pleasure of his ex, the new bride, like an actor playing a part on stage. The song couldn't end fast enough for him.

THE MEN STAYED behind to help Devon and Nick with some of the work not being done by the party planners or the caterers. Chairs were stacked and garbage bagged up. Every time Devon tried to do something, one of the SEALs prevented her.

It was good to see her laugh. It was good to just be with their own kind after the caterers and their helpers left. It was getting to be that Alex didn't feel he could have fun unless he was with his buds. He always felt on duty around the general public. Just something that came with the territory.

"Love it up here. So easy. Beautiful. Made for fun," Alex said. "Great place to relax."

"Looks can be deceiving," Mark added.

"He's right." Nick brought up something that recently appeared in the local news. "They found a Golden Gate Transit bus abandoned in Santa Rosa. People in our community and some of the retired cops I've talked to think it is terror-related. You gotta keep your eyes and ears open at all times, guys."

"Whatever happened with that property near Lucas' ranch up north? They ever find all those assholes who ran that terrorist training camp?" asked Alex.

"Devon said it went to auction, and another church group bought it," Nick answered.

"What the heck would someone want with a bus?" Jake leaned on his broom.

"Fill it full of explosives and park it on the Golden Gate Bridge, Jake." Coop's answer was smooth as silk. He didn't stop his quiet chair stacking to bother to look at any of them.

"A concerned neighbor made the call, and perhaps that thwarted the event," followed Nick. "Like I said, keep your eyes and ears open. They are looking for unexpected opportunities to create a huge loss of innocent life, and do it spectacularly. We're not DC or Coronado, but we're not immune."

But Alex had already had all those thoughts back in San Diego. It had been going on for weeks, ever since his divorce. Something was in the air. Strange people, sounds, bulges in pockets, whispers, dishonest glances—all these things were noticed. So were people with shifty eyes, or people who didn't look at you directly, or had a limp handshake.

It was late when they returned to the bunkhouse. Alex wanted to crash, but a couple of the guys stayed up to watch a movie. Mark said his good-byes and returned to Nick and Devon's house. Someone was in the shower. Alex threw himself on a bottom bunk and checked the time on his cell. He saw Sydney's text.

Are you having fun? How are your friends?

He placed the phone on his chest and looked up at the wooden slats of the upper bunk Cooper would be sleeping on later. She'd sent the text message nearly two hours ago. Should he return it? Wake her up? What were the odds she was also alone tonight? He hoped they were good.

Having fun, yes. But I think I miss you. Headed for bed. Nite Nite.

He hoped she didn't read anything else into his message. But then he wondered, what was he really trying to say?

CHAPTER 10

S YDNEY HEARD THE beep of her cell because she'd put it beside her on the nightstand. She wasn't sleeping well anyway. She sat up and cradled it, wondering if she should text him back, and decided not to do it. She wasn't sure yet whether she would try to contact him. It would be a miracle, but so much better if she could just run into him somewhere.

Where's your nerve, Sydney? Her internal mother was scolding her, which of course was going to keep her up further. She reached for a book, thinking it might make her sleep, and got snagged on it. Two hours later, she wasn't tired, but she knew she needed to get some sleep. The night before she'd had little, but no doubt about it, she was wide awake now.

"Fuck!"

Just admit it, Sydney. You want to see him again. You don't like it, but you do. That's why you came. Be honest with yourself.

The phone said 2:10 AM. More than likely he'd turned the sound off, so if she messaged him, he wouldn't get it until morning. Except he'd know she sent it in the middle of the night. And it would make her—*eager, Goddammit!*

Which was exactly why she balanced her phone on her thighs and sent her message.

Miss you too, Alex. Hope you're sleeping because I can't.

She didn't bother to wait for a response. Instead, she walked into the bathroom, washed her face, and brushed her teeth. While she was brushing her hair, she heard the ping and her heart leapt from her chest.

She nearly tripped on the way over to the bed.

Alex had texted, *Me neither. Wanna talk?*

If it's okay, she sent back. She wrinkled her nose at how dumb that sounded.

Just one second, let me wake up the guys and ask them.
No don't!

Are you kidding? I'd never do that. Headed outside to the porch. I'll call in 5.

She threw on a pair of sweats and a tank top. After pouring herself a diet coke from the minibar, she sat in the large, overstuffed chair in the corner by the window and waited. The minutes ticked by slowly. He called thirty-three seconds late. She let it ring twice first before picking it up.

"Hi, Alex. I'm sorry if I woke you." She toyed with the can of Coke. It was not caffeine free. *Crap.*

"Are you kidding? I thought I'd crash after the long drive, but now I'm wired."

"Tell me about it." She clapped her hand in front of her mouth. "Sometimes driving long distances does that to me too." She hoped she'd recovered well.

"We got up here in good shape. Our friends own this winery, and it's beautiful up here. There was a wedding."

"You were in a wedding? One of you guys got married?"

"No, but as it turns out, I knew some people here."

"Ah. And so all the flirting with the lovelies didn't make you tired?"

"That's a dumb question. Men don't get tired around lovelies, Sydney. You should know that."

She inhaled quickly. Yeah, that one served her right. "Of course. I forget." The pause was a little dangerous. "So, tell me about your friends, the part you can tell me, that is."

His chuckle sent a tiny zinger up her neck. "Not anything to hide here. Except the bride was my ex-wife. How's that for timing?"

"No way."

"Trust me on that, sweetheart. Had I known, well, I wouldn't have come."

"You're serious? Your friends didn't know about this?"

"Well, not like we were married long enough for them to meet her. I've only been here one time myself."

"So you're at a winery. Are you staying there, then?"

"Yep. They have a bunkhouse where people can come and learn about winery production, the cultivation of the vines and the soil, harvesting, crushing, that sort of thing. Sleeps eight. Except for the snoring, we're doing fine here."

"And you happened to stumble on a wedding for your ex? You have dark clouds above your head all the time, Alex? Or you just like to live dangerously?"

"Funny. I thought of you while I was dancing."

He paused. Sydney held her breath.

He continued, "I was thinking if you were here, I'd take you skydiving tomorrow. Seriously, that's what I was thinking when I was dancing. That's kinda nuts, huh? You down in San Diego and me up here."

It was her time to pause. It wasn't in her plan to tell him, but opportunity made it feel right, somehow.

"Did I say something wrong?"

Sydney recovered quickly. "Thing is, I got invited up here to visit my old roommate in college. So I'm actually staying in Santa Rosa."

"No fuckin' way."

"I didn't tell you because I didn't want to intrude on your plans. I drove up yesterday afternoon and got in late. That's when I texted you, Alex." She hoped her lie would hold.

"So where are you?"

"The Vintage, right downtown Santa Rosa."

She heard the long sigh and maybe the wheels turning inside his handsome head. It was probably a bad idea to tell him.

"Maybe we can meet for breakfast?" she added. She wanted to get him off the hook. "I've arranged to meet Carly at ten at Beach Inc. It's a huge volleyball complex over off Airport."

The heavy sigh was enough. It didn't matter what he said, because she could tell he wanted to see her, and that was all that was important.

"Let me see what I can do here. We're supposed to go over some plans. We've got some land to go see tomorrow—actually this morning, now. I gotta stay here. But tomorrow night?"

Sydney gulped down the rest of her Coke. She felt the tingle already coursing through her veins. "I'd like that. Now I really won't be able to sleep."

"Yeah, same here. You be careful around the caffeine, Sydney."

Too late. She'd heard all she needed to hear and didn't want to push her luck. "Promise. I'll be a good girl in the morning."

The deep chuckle in his voice was setting her on

fire. "Why don't I believe you?"

"No horror films on TV. I know because I checked. Not enough chocolate in the minibar, either."

"Oh, Sydney, Sydney, Sydney. Whatever am I going to do with you? Now you're making me hard as hell."

"Just hold that thought until tonight."

"Not sure I can wait."

"Music to my ears, sailor."

"Man, this is nuts."

"Welcome to my world."

"What's your room number?"

"Five Twelve."

"See you in fifteen."

He hung up. Sydney's pounding heart was making her breathless. She dashed to the shower, then afterward donned the little black nightgown she'd brought. She drank one of the bottles of water and then fingered the chocolate bar in the refrigerator but decided against it. She really wanted a run, but the stiffness from sitting so long in the car was beginning to evaporate. Some leg stretches and back bends helped, thirty pushups against the wall, and then…

OMG there was a knock on the door!

CHAPTER 11

H E BURST INTO the room without greeting, his hands under her nightie, her body pressed against him, her legs around his waist. She tugged at his shirt and pulled it off. His bare chest against her warm, shaking body was more than he'd hoped for tonight. Stolen moments. They wouldn't have the long luxurious time they'd had before. But this was just fine. It was urgent. It had to be done. It was what they both needed.

Her lips melted into him. Her little groan set him ablaze as he ran his teeth at her neck and bit her earlobe. Pushing her hands inside the front of his pants she found him. He helped her unbutton his jeans and slide them down off his hips. She grabbed his ass and pulled him into her, wrapping one thigh up and around his waist again.

The clothes had fallen away and at last they fell naked on the bed a tangle of arms and legs. Her hair was splayed over the pillows, the long lovely body of hers hungry, her sex wet with anticipation. She smelled of fresh soap and her arousal. His fingers slid over her thighs, reaching to that magical juncture between her legs as his thumb pressed her nub and he felt her lithe body arch under him. He owned her with that touch. He dipped his head down to taste her and she pulled his shoulders up, begging him. He was more than happy to do whatever she wanted.

He was hard as granite, sliding into her wet channel. She pulled him deep. He was lost in the feel of her lips against his, her little squeals and moans as he explored her with kisses. He started slow, rooting deep, encouraged and rewarded with her hands on his ass squeezing him tight. He picked up the pace as her eyes flashed open—the grin on her lips all he needed to see. She'd take all he could give, which spurred him on further.

FOR THE SECOND bright sunny morning in a row, she was draped across his body. If she was an addiction, he didn't want to be rid of the need. They didn't know each other at all. Had barely talked. He was used to having sex with lots of girls, one-night stands that were exciting, good for his ego, and probably good for theirs as well—or at least that's what he told himself. But this time, being with Sydney, all of a sudden he wanted to know all about her. He wanted to know where she got that drive, that extreme call to action to live full-out.

He watched her sleep, as she hugged his upper arm, burying it into her chest, looking like a little lost girl, like she'd never let go. Her face, with a soft crease between her brows, indicated perhaps she'd had a sudden bad dream. Maybe that's what wakened him. Carefully, he used his other hand, drawing the strands of brown hair from her forehead to watch her more closely. She clutched his upper arm tighter, rolling her hips against his thigh in her sleep.

He'd not been attracted to women who liked to dominate and possess. It had always been a total turnoff, no matter how stunning they were. Part of his DNA was not to be owned by anyone. When he found the SEAL brotherhood—working with the Teams—he discovered he'd been created for this job. These were the only guys he would ever trust.

It had been a sad fact of life that with all the intensity of his job and the life-threatening things he'd learned to handle, even the ones that haunted him and reappeared in dreams or whenever he closed his eyes— he'd never really wanted intensity when it came to women. The fair species were complicated and not to be trusted.

He'd give them protection and affection. No problem doing that. But he wouldn't go down that rabbit hole of emotions, and didn't want to be needed, and certainly didn't want to need.

He'd chosen his job because protectors were in short supply in this crazy world, and that was something he *could* do—to protect—even give his life for innocents. But he never wanted to go beyond the point of actual full-on engagement with his female relationships. Even his marriage with Brandy was half-hearted, and although he'd wished it could have been something more, it wasn't. Just wasn't.

But with Sydney, he wanted something larger, something more. He couldn't get enough of her. That had never happened before.

He cautioned himself as he laced his fingers down her backside. This was so damn quick and there was so much about her he didn't know. His first impression of her was that she was a total freak of nature. Could he now say that he really did trust her, or was it just the incredible sex? Was he just now awakening from a dreamy fog land of lust and the need to immerse himself in the warm waters of satisfaction and recreational enjoyment? It couldn't be anything more. Or was it?

Did it matter? *Yes, somehow it matters.*

As the light in the room brightened, he began to worry. His equilibrium was off. Perhaps storm clouds were about to appear on the horizon. It reminded him of the way early dawn looked overseas in the sandbox. On deployments, the question came with each pinkish-orange sunrise: "Is this the day?" He knew everyone thought about that.

What would his last day feel like? Would he recognize it? Would there be something in the air or a sound that would tell him his time was up? Would it be in a sandy divot without anything familiar but his brothers, or would it be in a soft bed like this, an old man, surrounded by his family? He'd never allowed himself the luxury of looking into his future.

Why was this coming up this morning? Was this bed so dangerous he should have these worrying thoughts? Dr. Death drinking at the side of the road, a hitchhiker waiting for him to pick him up? An unwelcomed partner, but an inevitable one?

Something had shifted these past two days, revealing a deep cavern inside. It lured him, like leaning too far over a high railing. Something here was dangerous. He just couldn't put his finger on it.

Next he knew she was rubbing her breasts against him, nibbling his neck, making his mouth water for her kisses. There was no question his body had surrendered to her in every way it could. Was there danger in the fact that she literally owned him? That he couldn't help himself around her? He would have to be careful not to let her know.

She'd been whispering, "…the way you kiss me, make love to me, Alex. I can't get enough. Do you hate me for this?" Why did she say that? Was she still asleep?

"Hate you? Absolutely not."

Sydney startled, and for a brief second he saw fear in her eyes, like she didn't know where she was. She quickly recovered and then it was gone.

What the hell was that about?

"Sydney. Are you all right?"

Her frown told him she wasn't happy with his question. "Of course. I'm fine." And then the cool veneer of her "I'm fine" mask disappeared. She became pliable again, soft, as she wrapped her legs around his thigh and pressed into him. "Never better."

EYE CONTACT WAS difficult over breakfast downstairs, which surprised him. He thought perhaps it was the distraction of the other people in the coffee shop. Alex was also getting texts from the team about his presence being required. Coop reminded him he'd promised to be back in time for their early meeting, and he intended to keep that commitment.

She played with her eggs but drank three cups of coffee. He raised his eyebrows as she took another long sip.

"You sure you'll be okay with all that coffee?"

"I'm not a child, Alex." The look she gave him was abrupt and cold.

"Just trying to be helpful. It's my nature to be protective."

The softness he'd enjoyed just a few minutes ago had vanished. He noticed she was about to blurt out something and then held it back, smiled, and patted his hand. "Thank you. But you know I'm a big girl." She watched his reaction and added, "Besides, there's no chocolate anywhere in sight. No zombies, either."

Her words coaxed a smile from him. "Good to know." The awkward silence between them still worried him. Something was brewing, or was it just his imagination?

Unknown territory. You are home. Drop it. Don't overthink this. He was well aware he could create a problem out of anything if he dwelled on it too much. Best to shed it like yesterday's clothes.

His phone buzzed again. He checked it and looked up at her. "Sydney, I'm afraid I have to go."

"Yes, and I have a workout to do with Carly."

"You want to get together later on? I have no idea when I'll be free. We're looking at this winery property today, and this morning doing some planning." He pointed to the phone. "They're basically waiting on me."

"I understand. Let's just see how things go today,

okay?" Again she didn't meet his gaze.

"That sounds good." He was compelled to say something rather than leave on such an awkward note. "Have I upset you?"

That got her attention. "Of course not, Alex. Don't be silly."

"All this happened so fast. Did I miss something here?"

"You mean the chitchat? The small talk about who we are and why we're here? That sort of thing? All we did was screw."

"And that's a bad thing? Is that what's bothering you?

"Not in the slightest."

Her answer surprised him, as he waited for more, but could see it wasn't going to come. The girl had demons. Powerful demons. He felt how tight she'd wound herself, masking something she wanted to hide from him. *What you think of me is none of my damn business.* That was sound advice, so he put that to work for him. But the hot and cold of her demeanor was worrisome.

"Well, if I offended you in some way—"

"Alex, would you fuckin' stop it? You haven't done anything to hurt me, so just quit this. Leave it alone. This isn't you. It's all me. Don't pry where you don't belong."

And there it was. Her shell of protection coming out like battle armor, telling him no matter what, she didn't need anything from him. "Well, I'd like you to know I had a wonderful time."

Her pert smile was efficient. "Me too."

He stood, but she remained seated, focused on her plate. He slipped his bag over his shoulder and heard her explanation.

"I'm going to have one more coffee, and then I'll be on my way too."

"You still staying over tonight?" he asked.

"Haven't decided." She didn't ask him if he wanted her to or mention seeing him tonight. Where was this distance coming from? Why was this so awkward?

"We'll touch base later on, then. Bye, Sydney." He leaned over, looking for a good-bye kiss, but when she didn't offer her lips to him, he gave her a chaste peck on the cheek.

The woman had demons. Perhaps she'd done him a huge favor.

ALEX GOT THE ration of crap he knew he'd get from the guys, who were just finishing up breakfast in the bunkhouse. Devon and Nick were clearing the table, with the help of several of the guys. Alex felt himself relax the instant he was back in this culture.

"Whoo-hoo, lover boy. Oh, lover boy!" Jake

crooned like the song.

"Shut the fuck up," Alex blurted. "You were the ones who set me up with her."

"Whew, I was hoping it wasn't Brandy, for some reason. The way your ex looked at you, all dressed up in her finest…" Cory continued his description of the way Brandy danced with him, exaggerated touching of breastbone to breastbone she'd done, which had embarrassed the hell out of him.

"Who do you think I am? You seriously think I could do something like that, you dumbass? I was just playing along. You fucking don't think I enjoyed myself, do you?"

"You say so," Cory continued to needle.

Alex wanted to grab him by the lavender T-shirt he was still wearing, and throw him on the compost pile. "I'm fuckin' *here*. That's all you guys need to know. Besides, I wasn't sleeping anyway. She *called me!* I didn't know she came up to see a friend." Alex shrugged trying to tone it down. A couple of deep breaths and he was right as rain. He poured himself a coffee from the machine on the counter and hoped they'd drop their line of questioning quick.

Coop leaned across the table on his elbows. "You wanna run that one by me again? She came all the way up here, what, just a coincidence it happened to be the same place you are? You're not reading anything into that? Ever hear the word *stalked?*"

"Not like that. Consenting adults and all that. I'm not sure we're gonna see each other for awhile, if you must meddle in my affairs."

Someone whistled. "Testy," Jake whispered.

"Hey, can we talk about something else? Besides, who could sleep with all of you snoring your butts off last night? I say you issue noseplugs, Coop."

"No kidding," Coop agreed. "Everyone wear ear-pieces tonight, and that's an order. The room is much smaller than we're used to. Surprised the windows didn't shatter."

With the table cleared, everyone was seated. Devon made more coffee.

Nick began, "So, I think you guys should look at this place Devon found. Not formally on the market, since the owner has just passed away. A nice forty-six-acre piece with a couple of okay houses on it. Vineyard has been allowed to overgrow two, maybe three seasons, from what we can tell."

"What does that mean?" Ryan asked.

"They have missed the last two years' prunings, so there's more than normal work to be done. It will affect the first harvest. And we also don't know the condition of the vines as far as disease. But we *do* know it produced pretty good Merlot when it was tended. They have a pond and a great well, which is always a plus in the valley." Nick handed out parcel maps and copies of the land description from the tax rolls.

"I'm getting reports in the next day or two," added Devon. "We've had to wait until after the funeral. The immediate family doesn't want the out-of-town relatives to know they want to sell."

"Don't they have to sign off on it?" asked Lucas. "If they're part of the estate—"

"They aren't in the will," answered Devon. "There are a couple of relatives hanging around for the reading, but we don't expect any surprises. We just want it clean and simple. The family is very private, and there are parts of the extended family that can get undesirable. At least that's what I've been told," answered Devon.

Alex noticed the tax rolls had the property valued at two million five. "Says here it's worth only two-five. Why are we supposed to pay four point two?"

"The tax rolls don't adequately reflect the true value, Alex. Happens all the time. We've seen a spike in sales prices, mostly because of some large buyers coming into the area."

"Why don't they go with them?" Mark asked.

"You can't be a vineyard owner up here without property disputes with the adjacent neighbors. Lots of issues. Water, drainage and grading, spraying. Vineyards are planted in different ways, some for deep watering, like the old ones were, others shallow, requiring more water. One of those big land owners is right next door. Marco Zapparelli. Ever heard that name before?"

"The movie director?"

"The one and only." Nick nodded. "And he's got a huge reputation for being really tough when it comes to negotiations. He rules by intimidation really. Doesn't care if he's liked or thought of as a good neighbor."

Devon added, "Of course up here, everyone smiles to your face while they stab you in the back. Maybe he's just putting everyone on notice, perhaps being more honest about it. Things are very competitive here and getting worse every year."

"So, when he gets wind of this property, he's going to have a cow that it wasn't brought to him," Nick finished.

"Entitlement," Mark whispered.

"Worse than that. He thinks he's the king of the whole fuckin' valley," Nick complained.

"See guys, size does matter," quipped Zak. "Although in this case, based on his track record and ours, he might be a bigger bully with his millions—"

"Ah, the pirate speaks!" barked Jake.

"Devon thinks it's billions, Zak."

"Like I was saying, even with those numbers, and

that kind of size, I'd still take our odds over his any-time. I mean, look what he does every day and look what we do?" Zak's eye patch was slightly crooked.

"Whoo-Ya, Special Operator Chambers," followed Coop.

Zak had been unusually silent all morning. Mark fist-bumped him. "Welcome home, brother."

CHAPTER 12

SYDNEY LINGERED AT the breakfast table as if she was hanging on to a memory of something fading away forever. The empty plates, water glasses, silverware and coffee cups were evidence two people had shared a meal, a conversation, and then a good-bye. She was hoping the longer she stared at it her body would react, but all she felt was the ice water in her veins, steeling herself from something she didn't want to feel. She was waiting for something. Waiting for warmth or some emotion to evolve. It never came.

Alex had left money on the table for breakfast without asking. She glanced to the view of the parking lot and thought perhaps she saw his Hummer exit toward the freeway entrance. Something melted inside, and she discovered a lone tear coursing down her face. Her cheeks were flushed and her hands were shaking. Glancing around, she looked for signs someone noticed, but found no one paying attention.

The thaw had begun. Before it got any worse, she exited the restaurant and walked down the wide, carpeted hallway to her room. The last time she'd walked down this runway she was holding the hand of a man. She wouldn't say his name. She refused to see his face or recall the feel of his touch. But her body knew it anyway.

The latch on her door clicked and flashed a green light. She walked back inside to the room still filled with the remnants of something deep. A place that bore witness to something she wouldn't allow herself to feel.

Their room, she corrected herself, coming dangerously close to that emotion again. The bed was coming apart. One pillow was on the floor. The evidence of a passionate play that had occurred between two people who—

Inside, she was caving. She sat down quickly, burying her face in her hands. She'd been cold to him, holding him off at arm's length. Refusing to let him inside her heart. It was her pattern. She'd done it over and over again without consequence, or at least not noticing one, if there was. But today, she was shattered.

The tears would not stop.

What is this? Get hold of yourself, Sydney. She didn't want to be pulled back to something dark, hiding in the emotions driving her tears.

Sydney straightened her back, wiped her face with her hands and then stood. With a wetted a washcloth, she dabbed her eyes, examining for signs of redness, and found none. Satisfied that the jumbled feeling inside wasn't visible on the outside, she pulled her hair back into a long ponytail. She brushed the ends, adjusted her sports bra, and put on her workout sweatshirt. With everything packed into her canvas workout bag, she filled the metal water bottle and tucked it into the netted pocket on the end.

Looking over the room again, she examined the evidence of their joining—the short story of their morning's passion and the path she'd taken to find him here out of the briar patch that was her soul. She'd found him, and he'd touched her. Again. It was dangerous. Risky.

And probably exactly what she needed.

Holding her key card, she hoisted her bag, and left the warm room behind.

Sydney considered checking out of the motel when the clerk asked her. She hadn't made her decision. She had to wait to see how the morning went, so she arranged a late checkout just in case, and promised to call later to let the hotel know for sure. The clerk was more than accommodating.

"You have until noon, perhaps later, so feel free to take your time. And, if I don't see you, thank you for staying with us at the Vintage."

Sydney noticed she was at the precipice again, stuck between leaving and staying. Time to set it all aside and put her game face on. Get her mind mentally prepared for a fierce conversation, hard workout, and driving herself to exhaustion and beyond. It was what always worked. It would certainly work this morning.

She arrived at the Beach Inc. complex twenty minutes early. Already the parking lot was filling with Suburbans as scores of high school girls' teams poured into the main gym, knee pads floating above their socks at their ankles.

Sydney walked through the heavy glass doors and heard the roar of voices, whistles, and team shouts. The air was cool, electric with excitement and purpose. She could feel the competitiveness hitting her flush in the face, and she loved it. Drank from it. Inhaling, she discovered she'd been holding up the entrance, so stepped aside to let several young players and their chaperones enter.

Carly had reserved a sand court, she'd told her. Sydney walked further into the space and noticed the two-story structure had perhaps a dozen traditional indoor courts arranged on both floors. Large expanses of glass divided the playing areas, with skylights bathing the whole interior in natural light. The state-of-the-art facility was impressive.

Several games were in progress. Sounds of whistles, the never-ending "sideout" and team cheers echoed throughout the huge structure. Parents and other team players sat on padded seats on risers instead of the standard metal or wooden benches Sydney was used to.

An Hawaiian-themed snack bar was down at one end of the building, near the four sand courts. Beach Boys and Margaritaville music boomed while two attendants in flowered Aloha shirts helped the customers. A short line of thin giraffe-like girls waited for smoothies and bagels for breakfast. Sydney had been one of them not too long ago. The squeal of an espresso machine pierced the air and surprised her.

Sydney smiled and shook her head. This was not what her growing up had been like. She'd played in hot, smelly gyms all over California, from brand new courts in the Central Valley to dingy inner city courts lined with graffiti and exploded toilets in the Bay Area and LA. She'd attended summer camps at colleges that didn't have gyms as nice as this one.

"Hey, bitch!" Carly's voice streamed across the room. "You ready to play, or are you going to go have a smoothie?"

Carly was a more compact version of Sydney's body type, with long legs and arms, but her height was well below six feet. Her blonde hair was tied up in pigtails, although it was hardly long enough to stay put.

The little golden strands looked more like horns. Her skin was paler, which told Sydney she hadn't been playing outdoor, even grass courts, recently. She was dressed in black, barefoot, and ready to play, holding a burgundy and white striped volleyball.

"Damn, Carly. This place rocks. Who owns it?"

"Believe it or not, a bunch of local businesses got a Title Nine grant. Some of the schools were pissed."

"I'll bet."

"But it's a nonprofit center. Major benefactor here in Sonoma County left them a ton of dough, and all they can spend it on is youth sports. So the schools can train here, have fundraisers. They even do birthday parties." She pointed to the second level where a bunch of balloons were tied to one of the open glass doors.

"Wow. I'm seriously impressed."

"They've done a couple more of these elsewhere. It's great for the girls, and the Beach has a couple of boys' and men's league teams as well."

"This is a serious draw for the community," Sydney remarked. "I don't think San Diego has anything close to this."

"Probably not. I think one's planned for L.A. Lord knows the schools don't have the money for anything these days. And the little private schools love it. They don't have to build a gym at all. I coach a public high school girls' team, and we have to ask each family to purchase a volleyball so we have enough for practice. It's *that* bad."

Sydney could only shake her head. "So that's what you've been doing, then? Coaching?"

"A little. It doesn't pay well enough to be full-time. I don't have a credential, so I'm always on the chopping block. They hire a P.E. or English instructor who can coach and I'm out of a job. Each year it's the same."

"You've done this more than one season?"

"Second year for Club volleyball. Starting second school year. They alternate, just like when we were growing up."

Sydney's mind was flooded with questions. "How are you going to work on the AVP thing if you live up here?"

Carly motioned for them to be seated at the edge of the court. She released the volleyball to the sand. "See, that depends. I can give up the school season if this works out. That comes up this fall. I have camps and some stuff here all summer long, but I'm replaceable. I have a few personal coaching one-on-ones, but"—she shrugged—"I'll have to give them up." She looked at her hands, then brushed them together, removing sand. "My assistant might be willing to take the varsity. I have to finish the Club season which ends here in a month."

"Okay. So what does it look like for us, then? Everything I see scheduled is down south."

"So we travel."

"*We?*"

She turned, extending her arm out, palm up. "This could be our training court."

"There are no beach games up here, right? I mean real beach."

"This is real." Carly scrunched up her nose.

"You know what I mean."

"There are a few facilities in the Bay Area. San Jose has a complex. They're building one in Santa Clara. For the beach scene, well, we'd have to drive a couple of hours south. Santa Cruz. There's also San Francisco, but the training could be here. Only difference, really, is we'd be watching the tournaments from onscreen, not live. We train for the qualifiers next year, Sydney. We give it a go and see where it takes us."

Maybe that would solve some of the other issues plaguing Sydney. She felt like she was in a fishbowl down south, everyone watching every move she made. The circuit knew she was looking for a partner. Knew it was a long shot she could get qualified to try out for the spots on AVP. She'd only get the points by winning qualifying tournaments. She wasn't aware of any of them indoors or many qualifiers up in Northern California. But she could get her conditioning done here. She could work on sponsors. She'd have a world-class place to train. She'd be out of the prying eyes of the field in Southern California.

"Okay, Carly," Sydney said as she lifted her sweatshirt. She drew down her pants and slipped off her shoes. "Let's see what you got."

They bumped back and forth over the net, chatting as they warmed up. In between short volleys, Sydney stretched, worked her shoulders, and practiced sprinting and jumping. She had no aches or pains today. Her game body had showed up this morning.

The two of them gave up the soft passes and started placing balls to make each other dive. After several good digs in the sand, Sydney felt the familiar sting in her knees.

Carly asked a couple of Sonoma State girls to join them. They worked across each other for a bit, then Sydney invited her back to her side, and they went two against two. Carly's hands were good. The players on the other side were young Sonoma State teammates who also worked at the Beach. Although competitive, Sydney had no problem hitting Carly's sets and getting a kill every time.

"Hey, old lady," Sydney shouted to her, "Your hands are still nice and soft."

"Told you, bitch," Carly hissed back and set another perfect ball for a kill.

They took several five-minute breaks, but Sydney wore them all out, demanding Carly get vocal. They had to work out their play dominance.

Close to noon, Carly held her stomach. "Man, Sydney, you don't play like you've been out for a bit, girl. If anything, I think you're stronger than when we used to play in LA."

"Been working out with Jack. He kicks my butt."

"Well, as long as that's it, he's good."

So the rumors had lingered. "We're not an item, Carly. Just want to be up front with you. That's all in the past."

"I got you," she said while continuing to catch her breath, leaning forward, her palms resting on her knees. "So, you wanna go get some lunch. The girls have teams they have to coach, and I think some reffing assignments."

Sydney checked her Apple Watch. "Good. I could use some food. I definitely need another water."

The place had premade sandwiches and chili, so it saved them from having to drive. And they could eat as they dressed without being hassled by the general public. Only thing that annoyed Sydney was the noise. Between the beach music and the whistle-blowing, it was hard to understand each other.

"Logistically, how do we pay for this space to train, Carly? I'm not made of money."

"How do you do it now, Sydney?"

"I have a little I've saved from my Dad's estate. I get my last chunk when I turn twenty-six. Enough to live on for a couple of years, if I'm careful. I'd rather invest it somewhere."

"Buy a house up here."

"Not sure I could qualify. I'm not on the tour yet."

"We could get you something here, if you wanted it. But I guess you'd have to rent some place. I have a studio. Maybe we shouldn't live together too, if we're training together. You know the pros and cons of that."

"I do."

"Way cheaper than San Diego rents. And if you work here, we can get our court times. Plus"—she held up a key on a ribbon key necklace—"we can train day or night. He who has the keys wins, in this case." Carly wiggled her eyebrows and with her pigtail horns looked ridiculous.

She made it sound very attractive. She knew Carly was capable of playing pro-level ball, which was dependent on training and working hard. She'd been one of the most competitive players she'd known in college.

"Why didn't you go on to play more afterward? What brought you up here?"

"My family's from here. I grew up with my mom in LA, but the rest of my family is up here." Carly continued on with her story. Sydney thought about her comment about parents living in two places.

Sydney knew about that. Growing up, she'd heard the fights at night between her parents. She used to will it to stop, covering her head with a pillow to drown out the sounds when she was in grammar school and beyond. By the time she began to play volleyball in middle school, the coldness had dug in and her parents never spoke to one another. She became the bridge between two icebergs.

And then came the divorce. Sydney had wished for, and now had, an end to the arguing. But she lost the company of her dad in the process. When her mother went on a serial boyfriend circuit, Sydney requested to go live with her dad. It became the best two years of her life.

Something familiar crept up on her shoulders and added dark weight. The hairs at the back of her neck stood out, then the tingling spread up to her scalp. In just a few seconds, her eyes filled with water.

"Hey, Sydney. You okay? Have you heard a thing of what I've been saying over the past couple of minutes?" Carly's hand was placed against Sydney's forearm. "Did I say something that upset you?"

There it is again.

"People keep apologizing around me today. Sorry, Carly. It started happening this morning."

Carly looked off to the side. "Yeah, the past hurts sometimes. Everything okay at home?"

"Home?"

"As in, your family, your love life."

How could she answer that? "There hasn't been any family for me since high school. I got a mom somewhere out there. Haven't seen her in over three years. Even graduation." Sydney paused because this was more difficult. "As for men? Fuck 'em."

Carly gave her a high five. "Damn straight, fuck them all to hell! I'm with you there."

She liked the way Carly picked up on the need for a change in vibe. Something unspoken between them had started already. It was a very encouraging sign.

"So I guess the next thing is, we gotta get you hired here. Would that make it easier for you to get a place to rent?"

"I'm guessing it would."

"Let's try it on our own in separate places first. If we have to compromise, we can always do the roommate thing. But we're going to train hard. We'll need our space. There are days when I'm not going to like you very much." Carly's playful lilt to her voice was a great way of covering some serious boundaries and guidelines.

"Well said. I can see you could be one major bitch."

"Damn straight."

Sydney liked her more than she thought she would. "Carly, I'm going to tell you exactly what I think of your play. I won't sugarcoat it."

Carly put her hands on her hips. "Another one of those, are you?"

"What does that mean?"

Her new playing partner put a cool towel to her face, then her neck. "What it means is, when you dance, I'll bet you lead."

No truer words were ever spoken.

CHAPTER 13

A LEX LIKED THE bright blue sky in Healdsburg, but the air was dry. Blue and white ocean and breaker views were replaced with bright green rows of vineyards looking like cornrows on a young girl. The gently sloping land could easily resemble a woman's body, all the curves and smoothed ridges and mounds, just like he'd seen in large expanses of African desert he'd flown over during deployments. Something about the land and its shape and shadows reminded him of a woman's curves and hollows. One *particular* woman.

A cool breeze caressed his cheek, whispering things as it swirled through the large plate-like leaves of the vines on the hillside they were hiking. Sections were bare or contained brown dying vines, while others remained dark green.

They'd spent the morning creating a very rough business plan, identifying all the decisions they had to make, who would be general partners, how the partnership shares would be divided and how decisions would be made. They left blanks for people's names to be inserted. They would need a chief executive officer, a chief financial officer, and a board of directors.

Next, Nick told them about the winery and how much work was required, especially taking over someone else's project mid-cycle. That led to the creation of a chief facilities officer position. Over lunch they discussed what qualifications would be needed for all these job descriptions without mentioning any names. They agreed to fill the positions in-house with the SEALs first, wherever possible. And they knew the CEO and CFOs would more than likely need to be someone who was getting off the Teams. These were not part-time jobs, so a salary would have to be paid, unless the people filling the slots were able financially to contribute their time, recouping it later on when they were making a profit. Nick and Devon would stay on as advisors, and perhaps partners too, depending on their cash situation.

As they drove up to the property, Devon looked in her element, still decorating her hair with bright red clips to hold what didn't hold up in a crystal comb. With her large belly and rosy cheeks, she didn't resemble the focused mindset of a star soft-pitch player or all-business attitude of the top-selling saleswoman in Sonoma County.

"I'd want to get Robert Minor from Davis to give us an evaluation," she said. "He'll be able to tell us if this is lack of water, or something systemic in the soil."

"Could it be that virus they talk about? What's it called?" Alex asked.

"Phylloxera, you mean?" Mark shook his head. "No, we got worse things here. Mildew, fungus. Those are our problems now." He stopped to examine a turning leaf, showing Alex a white powdery substance that could be scratched off with his fingernail. "When the old dead wood from the prior season isn't hauled away, it's a haven for pathogens. Here we got dead fruit, leaves, branches and other things blown in, all mixed together."

Jake asked the next question. "So the fact that the vineyard hasn't been properly tended means we have to understand what's here, what we have to fight."

"Identifying the enemy!" Coop confirmed.

"Yes." Mark walked down between the rows, kicking the dirt with his boot, stopping to pick a leaf here and there. He scraped the base of the vines with his toe. "Of course, one thing is for sure, this is prime Dry Creek Valley soil. Some of the most expensive vineyard land in the country. Perhaps the world."

"Let's go see the houses, shall we?" Devon asked.

Alex turned to Lucas and Zak. "You guys think you could live up here, do this?" They ambled over to the front door of the big house.

Lucas was first to speak. "I'm not ready to leave the Teams. You're not, are you, Alex?"

"Hell no. But someone will have to. That is, if we manage the money for the down payment."

"I'm game. Not sure how much longer they'll have me," Zak said. He had taken to wearing his black eye patch all the time, even though Alex knew he could sense some diffused light on occasion. The patch did more to hide the scarring around his eye than anything else.

"I know you're not the only one, Zak. Shoot, it coulda been me over there on the Canaries." Alex had always felt lucky his injury was to his leg, and not his face, like Zak. The mission was aborted without loss of life, except for the three would-be assassins against the Secretary of State. The public still wasn't aware how close they were to losing not only the Secretary, but several of the SEALs and State Department security team as well. Running a vineyard in beautiful Healdsburg seemed like a whole lot safer thing to do, and a pretty darned nice way to make a living.

But he wasn't ready to detach. Alex knew he'd fight a medical discharge tooth and nail.

They stepped on the large wraparound porch at the main house first. Built near the turn of the century, but Devon said it wasn't on the Historic Register. "Just some old guy who lived here forever. Think he bought it after World War II."

Inside, the home was still furnished with 1950's-style pieces right from a vintage House Beautiful magazine. The overstuffed upholstery still smelled of the man who was only dead a few days. A chill wiggled its way up Alex's spine.

"You get used to this sort of thing, Devon?" he asked her.

"What do you mean?"

"Looks like he's coming home anytime now. Just went out to do some shopping and will be back for some lunch and a nap."

"He's taking a nap all right," Cooper said.

The owner's pictures made one perfect row, lined up on the fireplace mantle. Old and yellowed, they revealed snapshots of a wife and children. Several other photos of graves and land without grapevines completed the display. As Alex looked around the living room, he didn't see any evidence of a feminine article indicating a woman had ever lived here.

They continued searching the rooms and timidly looking into closets. Most were empty. The master bedroom was different. The bare mattress looked out of place. The closet revealed gray and brown sweater vests, jackets hanging next to light tan pants and several wool plaid work shirts. Alex noted the man's boots were well worn, but clean, with two pair lined up next to one pair of polished black dress shoes.

"I see the shoes, but no suit to go with them," said Zak.

The two SEALs looked at each other and said at the same time, "He was buried in it."

Devon opened a dresser drawer. "Oh man, look at this."

Alex stood behind her, peering over her shoulder. There were several rolls of socks, organized by color, all rolled in the same direction.

"Okay, let's not open anything up until after the family has had a chance to inventory it," Devon added.

Despite the warning, Alex pulled on a broom closet knob at the end of the kitchen counter. The small storage area was nearly filled with stacks of brown paper bags, all folded in the same half fold, all facing the same direction.

How do some people live this way? Although Alex could appreciate the order, he couldn't understand the lack of anything entertaining or frivolous. An old black and white Mixmaster sat in one corner. The rolled Formica countertop was slightly spongy, containing swirls in turquoise, burgundy, yellow and black, and was edged in a one-inch metal strip tacked into place. He remarked how this could have been a June Cleaver kitchen just waiting for some cook from the 1950s to come home and prepare dinner for her family.

The TV in the living room looked like it was one of the first color models. No VCR or CD player of any kind. An unfamiliar electronics box on one of the open glass shelves was probably a record player.

"I'll bet there are some stories here. It would be kinda neat, if I had the time, to go through all his things and try to figure out who he had been and what he did."

All Alex got were blank stares and frowns from his Team buds. Devon's brow wrinkled. She pulled her briefcase onto the kitchen table and sat. Opening up her screen, she tapped a few keys and read before she looked up. "We have a couple of reports, but not the ones I was hoping for." She leaned back and cracked her back. "So, who's in and for how much?"

They went around the room, each SEAL giving their answer. Ryan and Cory were not sure they would go forward. Luke had gotten approval from Julie to pledge support. They didn't add Kyle, who had expressed interest. Several others might be added later.

"I got a signing bonus I'm due, but was going to use it for a house down payment," Alex added.

"Save it for the down payment, but we'll count you as in, without numbers," Devon responded.

She added up numbers she'd copied down. Lucas had no money to contribute, since he was in the middle of a nasty divorce, but mentioned he was willing to participate with labor. Coop noted his father-in-law was interested. Dr. Brownlee was also invested in Nick and Devon's winery as a minority partner. When it was all done, they had a commitment for nearly two hundred thousand dollars.

Alex whistled.

"That's not going to be enough," said Devon with a frown. "Not even 10 percent. On these deals, you will need 50 percent."

"So ask them, Devon," Nick insisted. "Tell them who we are. See if they'll take paper. You think there's any chance of that?"

"Not a snowball's chance in hell, Nick. I think they want the money. Maybe as a lease option, but honestly why would they do that? It ties the property up and all they get to keep is the option money if it doesn't work out. You're just buying a chance to bid on it in the future."

"At a set price, though," added Coop. "At least we know what we have to raise. Maybe that will give us a couple of years to do it."

"Couple of years?" Devon's grimace and near shout out echoed throughout the house. "I won't let you get into this with less than five to seven years as the option. Maybe some of you forget, you're still Uncle Sam's property. And you can't exactly order fertilizer and pay the help from the sand pit with PayPal."

"Yeah, the terrorists pretty much screwed up Pay-Pal for overseas stuff," muttered Mark.

Nick wouldn't give up. "Just ask them, sweetheart. See what you can do." He gave her a peck on the cheek. Everyone was smiling but their realtor.

"You guys are completely nuts," she blurted out.

Most everyone nodded and made some effort to verbally agree.

"You have no idea what you're getting yourselves into," she added with emphasis.

"Been there, done that," answered Jake.

"You forget, Devon, we all believed the bull our Naval recruiter told us when we signed up. So far, nothing has been anything like what he said." Lucas looked to his teammates for agreement and got it 100 percent.

"We could start working on the property as soon as they sign the agreement," said Alex.

"What agreement?"

"The one you're gonna create," he added.

She searched for a set of sympathetic eyes, turning from one man to another. At last she stood in front of her husband, Nick Dunn. "You can't let them do this, Nick."

"I'm not going to do it. *You* are. You just meet with the people. See where they're at, and then we'll see if we

can put some cash together and help with the details."
He took Devon in his arms. "Devon, you're good at
what you do. This is a walk in the park. We're the ones
doing all the work."

Devon collapsed into his chest, mumbling, "I never
thought you meant it, Nick."

"Come on, Devon," Zax interjected. "The least
they'd have is a place that would be better than when
they started."

Devon turned in Nick's arms, facing them. "You're
not going to prune and cultivate some forty-six acres
by yourselves, guys. You gotta hire that. And it costs
money."

"Yup." Coop was nodding his head. "Gents, I think
we've got some reading to catch up on. And Devon?
Please get that consultant over here ASAP. I know he'll
not do it for free, but we can cover that."

"Coop, it's likely to be several thousand dollars for
the preliminary study." Her eyebrows were raised but
Coop wasn't paying attention. Alex could tell he'd
made his mind up and so had the group.

"I think this would be a fun caper. Bunch of SEALs
going into the wine business. I can see it all now." His
palm moved across the air slightly higher than his
forehead, "Frog Piss Cellars."

That got a "Hooyah!"

Coop's cell rang. He stepped outside to take it in

private. Everyone inside could hear him greeting their LPO, Kyle Lansdowne. That meant that he was either on his way up, or they were on their way out.

CHAPTER 14

S YDNEY WAS ABOUT to sign the employment form. Her pen was poised above the document.

"You sure you don't want to think about it first? Go back to San Diego, try on all these ideas and make sure you're doing the right thing?" Carly was revealing her concern. Sydney noted how hard she was trying to hide it.

"I gotta do *something*, Carly. Timing's right. Someone asked me what I do. Asked me what makes me tick. I told them,"—she pointed down at the form—"this. I said I wanted a good partner, and then I wanted to focus on making it to the AVP circuit. I wanted to be the best of the best. I intend to be."

"Boy, you make your mind up fast."

"Feed me some caffeine and chocolate, and you'll see some rather swift mood changes too, my friend."

"I'm all in, Sydney. I think you can do it. Right now, I have nothing else either. So, who knows? Maybe we do this. Maybe we start something really big. Maybe we have an epic fail. You figure?"

"Does it matter?" Sydney said after she'd signed the form.

"I say we go until we can't any more. That's all." Carly's eyes were sparkling. Her bright smile was infectious.

"Let's find out where our limits are, Carly. Let's just test ourselves, find out how far we can go. It's not a win or fail thing. We just don't give up, until we have to." As soon as she said it, Sydney knew who she sounded like.

"I like that attitude." Carly picked up the signed contract and put it in the general manager's in basket. "Done!" she said as she swept her hands together.

The day was coming to a close. "You staying at the Vintage again tonight?"

Sydney's internal smile warmed her belly with excitement. Memories. She would sleep soundly with the double session workout today. "Yes, ma'am. Are you starved, because I sure am?"

"I could eat a tire right now."

"Why don't you change and meet me at the Vintage? We can walk a couple of blocks to some restaurants. You know the area." Sydney might have offered to eat something simple at the diner at the hotel, but didn't want to be reminded of this morning's breakfast with Alex.

Carly agreed. They fist-bumped and went their separate ways.

When she returned to the motel, Sydney greeted the front desk clerk and headed to her room. In the back of her mind was concern about whether or not to contact Alex. She had hoped her decision would be clearer by the end of the day.

The workout had been grueling. She'd eaten healthy, not skipped her lunch. That was usually all it took to get her head level. But when it came to Alex, something inside her was ringing off the wall. An unanswered phone at an abandoned phone booth.

Her room was clean, but she could still smell the pheromones and visualize the look of them on the bed, as if she were gazing at a mirror while their bodies blended, went on that fantasy ride, trying to get as close as possible, indulging in the intensity without holding back. These sexual workouts were like fuel to her soul. Instead of settling her thoughts, the encounters brought energy and life to her world.

So, it was a conscious choice. *Do I look for that recharge of my batteries or go for logical forward planning?* She wondered if Alex thought that way, and realized perhaps it worked in him the opposite. In a firefight, there certainly would be the emotions of just staying alive in a dangerous place, saving each other.

But through the fog of war, he was trained to think. Trained to use what they'd taught him. She could see why SEALs would have trouble assimilating into the "real" world, whatever that was. He was addicted to being the best Alex he could be, the killer machine.

Sydney had heard it said many times a good coach could tell which team was going to win by the intensity of their warm-up or their training for the week. She knew it was impossible to hide a lack of training, especially playing against a good opponent who would exploit the weaknesses they discovered. If her opponent saw she had difficulty with one particular type of serve, guess what she would see over and over again? That's if the opponent was talented and had the control to exploit it.

So too with Alex and the SEALs. It wasn't the superior equipment or firepower. It was their training, and something else—their mindset. She'd seen those poor guys down at the beach getting wet and sandy. Some of them were focused, others were checking out the pretty girls and showing off when they thought they could get away with it. But the ones who were going to make it could have been surfing on an iceberg like a polar bear, soaking up what little solar heat came from the crystals of ice reflected. They took advantage of every chance they had.

She sat on the bed and searched the empty walls of

the motel room. She had a lot to do. She had to go back and pack, say good-bye to some friends, deal with Jack, gather her things in a rental trailer, and get herself back up here in two or three days' time, find a place to live, and start her new job. There wasn't a lot of room for second guesses. Overwhelming.

So maybe the good-bye she needed to do with Alex needed to be done in person, up here.

And, unless she was crazy, Sydney picked up that he expected her to contact him before she left. Maybe he was already on his way home too.

Am I ready for this?

The answer was a resouncing, *yes!*

CHAPTER 15

COOP BROUGHT EVERYONE together in a huddle. Devon walked outside with two of the heirs, both granddaughters of the late Mr. Santos.

"That was Kyle just now. Danny has gotten word Ali's paperwork has been stalled. As most of you know, he's been trying to bring the little guy here to the States."

Alex remembered seeing pictures of the little brown-haired boy and his poor father, the former Iraqi captain, who had lost the rest of his family, but deserted to spend his last days trying to protect his four-year-old son.

"I thought he was already at the orphanage north of Bagdad," Luke said. Alex and the others nodded in agreement.

"Perhaps you didn't hear the news. Parts of the city have been taken over by ISIS and other renegade fighters. The UN workers have been ordered to leave,"

Coop added.

"So what happens to the kids?" asked Alex.

"We don't know. I'm afraid once the aid workers leave, they'll be on their own."

"Those *assholes*," shouted Jake.

"Kyle says we're to get our butts back down to San Diego tomorrow. Alex, you, Lucas, Jake, Mark, and I have been given the opportunity to volunteer for 'Operation Ali Baba.' Luke, Ryan, and Cory, you may be needed so we're asking you to return home with the others too." Coop walked over to Zak, placing his hands on the one-eyed SEAL's shoulders. "Zak, you've been ordered to stand down for this pending further orders."

"I'll help in any capacity that's given me," croaked Zak. Alex could see he was emotional about not being selected to serve even in a support role.

"You'll be staying in San Diego, Zak. But we'll see if we can get something for you to do. Or you can stay here."

"No, I want to go with the rest of my team."

Nick stood next to him and placed an arm around his shoulder. "We need you to stay here, Zak. They can reach you by phone just as well from here as San Diego."

Coop nodded. "You're still cleared for time off up here. I say you stay and help Devon." He examined the faces of the rest of the team. "If any of these guys want to start talking vineyards, soil analysis, escrow instructions, or financial statements, you're our go-to guy. Got it?"

Zak accepted his fate and agreed to stay behind.

"Danny must be beside himself," whispered Mark. "He's going too, right?"

"Yes. On his way. He and Luci are building a house on the Res. He, T.J., Fredo, and Rory will meet us in San Diego tomorrow. We can catch a flight out of Schulz Airport early tomorrow morning, then fly out oh-one hundred Monday morning for the pit. Kyle and the staff are making all the arrangements."

"Or we drive. Fuck, I'm leaving tonight," said Mark. "I could use some company to take turns navigating so I can get some sleep. I don't want to wait until tomorrow. I won't have any time to say good-bye to Sophia."

"If we fly out, how do we get the trucks back home? We gotta drive, Coop," said Ryan.

"I need to run it by Kyle first, but if you want to, don't have a problem with that. You'll get home before we will. Who wants to go with him if it's approved?"

Everyone raised their hands, except Zak and Alex.

Coop walked up to Nick. "Sorry, man. That work party's going to have to be delayed some."

"Hey, you guys, this is important, way more important than the winery deal. Devon will try to work her magic while you're gone, and Zak and I will see what we got when you get back," Nick said.

Coop and the rest of the team focused on Alex. Coop asked, "So what's up with you?"

"Coop, if it's okay, may I fly back tomorrow morning? I can say my good-byes up here. I'll leave my truck with Zak here, although you sonofabitch put a scratch on it with your one-eyed driving and I'll personally come back and poke out your other eye."

The light-hearted laughter was welcomed and eased some of the tension of the upcoming mission.

"Okay, lemme get Kyle back on the phone. And one of you guys has to ride with me. I'm not driving that whole distance without some shut-eye. Lord knows we won't get much rest bouncing around in that box of rocks getting over there."

Devon was shaking hands as the two daughters looked through the doorway at the group of SEALs in the kitchen. One of them smiled and waved, which was returned by several of the guys.

Devon burst through the ten-light door with a confident smile on her face. "I have great news!" When she saw a lack of excitement on the long faces of her husband and the rest of the team, she asked, "So who died?"

"We've had a change of plans, sweetheart." Nick

took her hand. "Everyone's got to go back to San Diego."

"What, now? How will we get a contract signed?"

Nick pulled Zak to him. "We've got the bossman here. He's staying behind to help put together the deets, just in case we can."

Devon was searching for some clue as to what had occurred while she was outside doing her sales pitch to the two girls. Nick gave a pleading glance at Coop, who decided it was okay to let her know a little bit about the mission.

"Little Ali, the boy Danny has been trying to get cleared to come here, is in trouble. We're being called on to help rescue some aid workers and the kids who stayed behind. That's all I can tell you and you can't say anything, Devon."

"No problem."

"I would like your good news, though," Alex asked.

"The heirs are several months away from making a decision on what to do with the money, working with accountants and attorneys and such. Since they know it will take time to do your proper research, and they're not ready yet to part with the place, not to mention clean everything out, they will entertain an option to purchase, first right, for a nominal fee."

"How nominal?" Coop asked, ever the frugal one.

"Only fifty thousand dollars. They'll give a two

year, with an automatic two year extension for an additional fee."

Alex heard several whistles. Coop swore, "That's nominal?"

Zak began to lighten up. "Shoot, I think my wife's father and his buddies on the force would be interested in helping out with that one. They could raise that kind of dough, no problem."

"Zak, why don't you have her come up, and you can stay with us?"

Coop interrupted. "Going to make that call," he said as he exited to the outside.

Alex mulled over his possibilities in case Kyle nixed his request. He could just leave the truck for Zak to use and fly back to San Diego or ride back with Cooper. There were a lot of things about the mission he had questions about since he hadn't been involved in the original rescue of Ali a year ago.

Or he could attempt to see Sydney one more time. Only question was, would it be smart to call her or let her call him? She'd been obvious she wanted her space. And maybe she was already planning to return or had started the trip back. He knew he had to find out.

Coop walked back through the kitchen doorway. "Okay, Alex, you're set to fly home tomorrow at oh-six-hundred. Don't be late. The rest of you, we get back to the winery, load up, and leave."

Devon locked the door behind them. "We never got to see the guest cottage. There are outbuildings too. I'll show Zak tomorrow, and we'll send pictures to all of you. Maybe do a podcast?" She smiled and patted Zak on the back.

"Yeah, we'll make a YouTube video," answered Zak, who appeared to be warming up to the idea of staying behind.

ALEX GAVE COOP some gear he wouldn't be able to bring on the plane. He never went on the road without packing. He doubted the small airline and airport would be forgiving of him bringing any firearm on the plane.

He walked into the bunk room, sat on a creaky chair, and called Sydney.

She picked up, with music and the sound of a crowd in the background. "Hold on a minute, Alex. I can't hear well."

He waited. His heart was pounding in his chest.

"Okay. Sorry. I'm having dinner with my friend."

"Oh, good. That work out for you, then?"

"Yes. We're excited about working together."

"That's great, Syd. Say, I just wanted to say good-bye. We're leaving for an overseas gig tomorrow, and I'll be gone for a while. I know I wasn't supposed to call you—"

"No, it's all right, Alex. I'm glad you did."

"Well, I wasn't going to. I was going to give you lots of space, which it sounds like you need, especially now that you're focused on your training."

"Thank you."

The silence hung between them. It was almost as heavy as the lump in his chest.

"I appreciate your restraint, Alex. I really do. I've made some plans. Maybe after dinner we could talk? If you're not busy."

"You want me to give you a call then?"

She paused. "I—I know if you're leaving tomorrow you'll want to get some rest, and I wouldn't want to keep you up—"

"Come on, Sydney. Nothing I'd rather do than talk to you again, and I think you know that about me by now."

"Are you free in person?" He heard her heavy breathing, belying her nervousness. It sparked his need all too quickly.

"I can be free in person. Is that what you'd like?" She didn't answer him, so he persisted. "Sydney, you gotta tell me what you like."

"Well, if you're going to be gone, maybe a proper good-bye? So yes, I'd like to see you."

"Me too." He worried that he sounded too urgent.

She paused. Her words were calculated, careful,

well crafted.

"Well then, I'll try to keep the talking down to a minimum."

"Promise?"

"Maybe."

"That's good enough for me, sweetheart. I have to be at the airport at 5:00 a.m."

"That should give us just about enough time. Barely."

"I can hardly wait. How much longer will you be with your friend?"

"Stop by and I'll introduce you two. You should meet Carly. We're at the Mexican place on the square."

"Near the motel?"

"That very one."

"I'll see you soon, then."

Hanging up, he wondered what doorway he was entering tonight. And was it a good idea before stepping through the gates of Hell?

But that's what life gave him, and he'd always been one to make the most out of what he was given.

The future was always uncertain, but tonight was a pure gift.

CHAPTER 16

SYDNEY KNEW ALEX had entered the restaurant and was approaching her back from the reaction on Carly's face. Her eyes got huge, her chest got blotchy, and her normally composed friend fiddled with an errant strand of hair at her temple.

"Um, there's some really big guy coming toward us, Sydney. Tall, dark, and dangerous."

Sydney smiled. "I think you're about to have an Alex encounter."

"Holy shit," Carly said as she retreated to her margarita and kept her gaze down.

He sat down next to Sydney, putting his arm around her shoulder, drawing her sideways into him, and giving her a kiss on the cheek. He left his large hand at the base of her skull to massage the upper vertebrae there, which warmed her all over.

She worked up the nerve to turn and face him. His soft eyes said all the right things. "Hey you," she whispered, with a smile chaser that was returned.

Alex abruptly drew his attention to Carly, extending his hand over the table. "Name's Alex Kowicki. So you must be Carly, is it?"

"Nice to meet you, Alex," she said as she took his hand and then withdrew. Her scrutiny going back and forth between Sydney and Alex telegraphed she was piecing together clues of a very strong sexual pull.

"Well, I imagine I'll be seeing more of you, then," Carly started. "Alex, you live up here in Sonoma County?"

"No, ma'am. San Diego. I'm in the Navy."

"Of course you are!" Carly's little laugh was suddenly sharp and a little too loud for the room, turning a couple of heads. "Well, I'll let the two of you get on with your evening, then. Sydney and I are just about done, right?" She ended her statement with raised eyebrows and bowed head in Sydney's direction.

"Yes, I'll touch base with you tomorrow, before I leave."

"Leave? You're leaving?" he asked her.

"Yes, I've decided to move up here and train with Carly. She's got me a job and everything. I'm going home to get my things, and then I'll be looking for a place to rent."

"Oh, and she can stay with me until she does. Not to worry," Carly piped up.

"I see." He was looking deep into Sydney's eyes without a trace of a smile.

"That's why I thought it would be a good idea to have a talk before you go back, Alex," Sydney whispered.

"Oh! That's why then." He smiled, taking her hand in his. Unashamed to show affection for her, he kissed her knuckles. Peripherally, she could see Carly had closed her eyes briefly. His lips were warm, lingering slightly longer than a normal kiss. She felt the tip of his tongue press slightly between her index and middle finger. She focused on his wet lips and the tiny flare of his nostrils as his thumb rubbed persistently on the underside of her palm. She had totally surrendered to his touch. Again.

"Okay, that's my cue." Carly's voice was laced with a nervous edge. She stood, and Sydney did the same, giving her a hug.

"I'll call you tomorrow, Carly. Thanks for everything."

Alex was picking off Sydney's plate.

"We can order you something," she said, watching him inhale the food.

"Nope, I like yours here." He smiled between bites. "You okay with this?" he asked pointing to her near-empty plate with his fork.

"I'm totally okay with this. I like watching you eat."

He winked at her, grabbed for a tortilla chip and, after piling on more salsa than she thought possible, lobbed it in his mouth. He wiped his lips with a napkin and stared at hers. "You ready to talk?"

"Whenever you are."

"Let's see how far we get. You want another margarita?"

"Sure." Her insides were melting like butter.

Alex stood and drew their waitress over, ordering a large strawberry margarita. "We're sharing," he said as he scooted closer to her. "So, Sydney, you've been a busy girl in the last few hours. Tell me about your plans."

"Carly has some really good hands. Her setting skills are great, she digs as good as I can, and she picks things up quick. She'll be a good partner for me."

"That's cool. What else?"

"There's this first-class facility here. She coaches a couple of teams, and then works at the gym. We'd have practically unlimited court time, so staying up here, especially after she got me a job there, seemed like the logical choice. I've decided I'm moving. The choice was simple."

"Sounds well thought out. You can tell that much from one workout with her?"

"No, we've known each other, played against each other in college. Otherwise, yes, you'd call it an impulsive decision. But being up here, out of the big scene down in Southern California, is healthier for me."

He was watching her. She could feel his eyes on the top of her head as she examined her fingers.

"And what's the downside?"

"Well, not being around the circuit live, maybe my intensity will wane?"

"You?"

She laughed with him. "Well, I guess I could stock up on Junior Mints, caffeine and popcorn."

"But stay away from the movies, sweetheart. At least until I can come up for a visit."

"Another downside too. I wouldn't get to see you as often."

"Well, as it turns out, we might be coming up a bunch more when we get back from the sandbox. Looks like we've located a property to purchase. A rundown winery property. I'll be coming up now and then to lend a hand if they go through with it."

"That would be fantastic." Sydney traced over some of the banded tats on Alex's forearm. She walked with two fingers the three-toed track marks inside his right arm. "What are these?"

"Just something we do on Kyle's team. We all get frog prints. You know, we're frogmen and all."

"Right." Her fingers touched his chest. He placed his hand over hers and drew it over his heart.

She could tell he wanted to say something but wasn't quite comfortable with it.

"So you leave tomorrow. Can you tell me what you'll be doing or how long you'll be gone?"

"This isn't our normal workup. Usually we train, then go, and afterwards have a few weeks of light duty stateside. This is something that came up, sort of an emergency mission, involving a friend."

"Okay." She could still feel his heart beating as he hadn't removed her hand from his chest. "But it's dangerous?"

"Dangerous everywhere, sweetheart. Getting worse by the day. One of the guys you met had his lady kidnapped by a terrorist group up north over a year ago."

She shivered at the thought of the loss of life happening on the other side of the world.

"Nothing for you to worry about. We got this."

"I've heard that line a few times in movies recently."

"Yeah, those are the cocky bastards who go running in until the zombies get them." Alex's grin was infectious. She found herself laughing at the dark humor.

"I'm glad you'll be here with your friend. Just keep your eyes and ears open at all times I wish I had time to drive back to San Diego with you and bring you back, but no can do."

Sydney lowered her voice to a sultry whisper. "Well, I have other ideas how we can spend the time together. None of them included riding in my van or your Hummer for ten hours."

"Well, we agree on that, for sure."

ALEX DROVE HER to the Vintage only two blocks away. Sydney noticed her mood was calm, the result of a good day's physical exertion. Her emotions were between the lines. Even her heightened arousal and sense of anticipation didn't take her off kilter. It was the first time she'd felt this way around Alex.

She noticed little things, like the way he sat, removed his shoes, and took his shirt off and laid it over the easy chair carefully. His jeans were folded on the seat. His American flag boxers were also folded. His T-shirt was draped carefully over the arm of the chair, and then smoothed over by his palms.

He hadn't looked at her while he did these things, or watched her while she undressed. When at last they were both naked, he on one side of the bed and Sydney on the other, they both paused without saying a word. His muscular body had a number of scars and tats she'd not noticed before in their urgent lovemaking of the last two days. His arms were longer than she'd remembered. The little finger on his left hand angled to the side, a little out of joint. He had a crescent-shaped purple scar over his upper thigh, dotted with evidence of old stitches now healed. A fresh bruise and scrape was on one knee. His body had worked hard in his nearly thirty years. His years as a Navy SEAL had taken their toll.

She had more delicate scars, like the surgery she'd had to her left elbow, a tiny scar from being smacked in the face with a glass wall when she tried to play handball and dove like she did on the beach. She had a crooked toe to match his little finger, but Alex wouldn't be able to see it.

She pulled her ponytail band from her hair, which was the signal for him to slip under the sheets. His tanned torso lying back against the stark white cotton pillowcases nearly took her breath away.

Whatever she'd done to come to this place, this right now, she was grateful for. Life was uncertain. Love could be cruel. Expectations were the darkest and sometimes the ugliest emotions in her soul. But tonight, she had none of them. She was on equal footing with this man who was a trained killer, a man who knew how to win and adapt to his environment. And he was waiting on her, watching her now as she pulled back the sheets, sat, and slipped her feet under the covers.

In seconds her body came to his like a heat-seeking

missile, merging with the length of his thighs, and she felt his coarse hands slipping over her body. The taste of his careful, slow kisses sent a shiver down her spine and nearly brought her to tears. He covered her body, resting on his arms at her sides, sliding her long bangs from her forehead, dipping now and then to nibble under her ear or extract a wet kiss with the promise of something deeper. Her fingers touched his cheekbones, and she curled her other fingers behind his ears and then laced through his hair at the back of his head. She brought him forward to speak to his lips.

"You asked me, Alex, who I am."

He dipped his head lower to kiss her, but she placed her fingers between their lips.

"I'm that shooting star in the night sky. Going on a long, long journey, on my own trajectory. And then I ran into you. And it feels like I've planned it this way."

He chuckled. "Game of chance. Dangerous and beautiful, an exciting combination."

"Yes," she said. "Even our first date was a gamble. Arranged by others."

"Amazingly so." He was moving against her, angling his hips as he kissed her from her collarbone to just under her ear. And then he whispered, "Sydney, you promised."

She searched for the answer he was seeking. "Promised what?"

He continued nibbling down her neck, across and under her chin, holding her arms over her head with one of his hands, tucking his hip beneath her left thigh, raising it slightly over his waist so he could find her and slip home. But just before he did, he answered her question.

"You promised not to talk too much."

CHAPTER 17

I N THE EARLY morning hours, there is truth and honesty, Alex thought to himself. The distractions of daytime and the clashing of needs versus the time available, the sorting and choosing of tasks for specific purposes—all that was washed away in the early morning, honest hours of the new day.

Here, rising from the stupor of a love-lust indulgence, his heart still racing with the intensity of their lovemaking, becoming as close as he possibly could be to her, this magical angel who had stumbled into his life, he had no defense. Nor did he seek cover. He was as engaged as he could be without wearing her skin. But even that he would do if it would bring him more of the pleasure of her being.

It was strange that he'd never realized the hole that was there in his heart, even with the touching demonstrations of human kindness and cruelty he'd experienced being an elite warrior. He'd played his role, more as a means to test his own limits. And now he had something too that could be sacrificed, something larger and more important than his own life.

This time he was going off to battle with the taste of her still sweet on his tongue, something that could be taken away from him forever. Something he never wanted to lose. It was more than the loss of his favorite mutt growing up, or the girl he didn't get, or the loss of his cousin in the Twin Towers, the early passing of his grandmother, the number of times he'd sworn at his sister Joanne even though she told him he was going to Hell, and the father he never knew. Those were also regrets, scars that certified he was a human being and could feel, could love, could lose.

But never before had he willingly lifted his soul out on a silver platter and handed it to someone else to take, to discard, to not nurture or pay attention to. It was that trust in the space between where she was and where he was. All he wanted to do was show her, tell her that it had never happened to him before.

For the first time in his life, he didn't have a plan. This had never been a goal of his. Wasn't a direction he consciously moved towards. But he was here now. And in his arms was the most precious thing he'd ever experienced. It wasn't just the sex, although that was part of it certainly; it was the unrelenting life force of this lady who knocked him on his butt and made him look at his life as something incomplete without her.

And everything that had occurred up until now was just the path leading him here.

He wished she was awake, but he enjoyed the warm sweaty feel of her body halfway laying across his. She liked to be on top, he mused. His eyes watered as he felt her stir.

Then he'd be her foundation. He'd be her rock until he could no longer hold the bounds of his being together before letting it all fly off to Heaven.

Her forefinger encircled his nipple. Her breathing became deeper as her lithe body awakened to his day, charming every place her skin touched his. What a glorious way to wake up. Warriors throughout history were sent off to battle by the women who loved them, but none so grand as he was being sent by today.

"You're deep in thought, Alex. Share a little sample with me," she whispered and then kissed his chest, exploring with her tongue.

"I hesitate to say anything. I admonished you for talking too much last night." Her head popped up, and they shared a friendly smile. "And I so enjoyed the punishment, Alex."

"I need you to speak into my phone, so I can hear you say my name. I want to play it like a hundred times a day."

She arched on her elbows, bracing on his torso. His

fingers luxuriously laced up and down her back, smoothing over her ass. The contour and feel of her body was even better than the view.

Sydney had been studying him. "So I pose the question again, talk to me, Alex."

At first he couldn't speak. She lightly traced the ridge of his left ear, slipping her three fingers down his cheek, following his jawline and then over his lips. Her thumbs moved upward, gently rubbing his eyebrows. She squeezed his earlobes between her thumb and first two fingers. He could feel her nipples harden against him as she inhaled what he was thinking and could not find words for.

She angled her head and smiled again. "You can't can you?"

It was true. He had no words. He drew his hand up to cover his eyes, and she captured it. "Then let me say it."

His breath hitched like he'd been exposed to a cold wind. He waited for what she was going to say next, hoping it would be something that wouldn't shatter their last morning together.

"I don't want you to go. I don't want this day to end with a good-bye."

He clutched her buttocks, bringing her into his groin. He quickly slipped from under her and pressed her into the bed, his hands on her face as he kissed her smile of pleasure. "Say it again, Sydney. Tell me again."

"I don't want you to go."

Could it really be? Could this be the dreaded "L" word creeping into his world? Is that what this feeling was? She was already a part of him, the *best* part of him, the part of him that would ache like the dickens on that airplane all those hours while he missed this, the part of him that would make him crash through anything and any obstacle to come back to her. His woman.

He angled himself to enter her as if it was the first, as every time was for him now. The words were there, but his tongue wouldn't cooperate. There was a frog in his throat. He arched upward as she pulled him inside her, her fists grabbing the flesh of his butt cheeks. He looked down on her smiling face as the wash of wonderful flesh on flesh consumed him. "Sydney," he whispered.

She waited with that knowing smile, matching his movements but her eyes remained tightly fixed on him. She knew. She knew what he so desperately wanted to say.

Her warm channel hugged him. Her thigh slung over his hip, reminding him how much he needed her body to show him how to be a real man.

She was shattering beneath him, almost as if she were suffering bravely. It was tears she was holding back. They thickly rolled from the corners of her eyes, onto the pillow with dark gray stains. Her body began to shake, but she wouldn't stop looking at him.

Was he somehow hurting her, while his body demanded satisfaction? He could not stop.

His arms slid between her warm, beautiful back and the mattress, as he pulled her up into his arms. She let her head roll back as if she was in a freefall. He held her shaking body wishing he could find the words he knew she wanted to hear.

His seed came with satisfying grace, so much more intense now that he knew whatever he felt between them, she felt the same.

He watched over her, tenderly kissing her while her orgasm pulsed, wearing her body out like a rag. He gently guided her home, back to the here and now, back from the peak of their passion to the real world where they stood side by side, as the perfect team.

He'd defend her to the ends of the earth. Nothing in the world would keep him from coming home to this woman. No price was too great to pay, no sacrifice too dear. She had opened up the future to him, and he knew he would never be the same.

CHAPTER 18

THE TEAM ASSEMBLED in their SEAL Team 3 hangar, even the men who were staying behind. Kyle had asked that they bring every extra piece of firepower they owned, since they'd be riding military all the way and wouldn't be under the restrictions of commercial travel. There was government issue, and then there was every man's personal tastes when it came to weaponry. It also indicated to the men that for this fight it was important to use what they were comfortable with and accustomed to using—a sure sign they were in for some rough times.

Alex sat beside Cory and Ryan, his other roommates. Luke sat in front of them with two other team guys who were also not going on the mission. Coop and Fredo sat in the front row near Kyle.

Danny Begay was not his normal stoic self, nor was he sociable. The Navajo weapons and explosives specialist sat all alone in the last row of their little theater while Kyle went over the drill.

"Begay, you with us?" Kyle barked.

There was no quick response on Danny's part. Alex could only imagine how the man felt. He'd been trying for nearly a year to get the little boy out of Iraq after the sacrifice of his military father. Alex knew Danny considered it a debt to be paid in full and would not rest until it had been.

As SEALs, they could cut through anything and be the ones to "get 'er done," as their training required. But cutting through bureaucratic red tape was something they had trouble with. No one could understand how anyone could object to Ali and the other orphans in the temporary shelter coming to the States to families who would give them a new life. While everyone held their breath and waited, the children were looked after by some UN aid workers. And now something was seriously wrong with that arrangement. Alex was about to find out how wrong.

Danny looked up slowly, but kept his crooked slouch position, one boot on the crossbar of the chair in front of him, his hands in his lap fiddling with a bright red slingshot. The man was legendary how accurate he was with that thing, especially with the stainless steel balls he carried. But he could be just as accurate with a pebble or piece of glass. With his hunting skills, he was the most lethal killer the Team had when it came to perfectly silent hand-to-hand combat. When he threw knives, Danny never missed.

Ali was Danny's project and although he sat alone, the whole Team was there to make sure this time Danny got to bring Ali back.

"So here's the problem with our mission. The kids and aid workers—and we think there are four workers and ten children now, down from twelve kids—" Kyle flashed a stern look back at Danny who appeared as if he wanted to punch someone "—so we go in not knowing who's still alive. Our intel has told us only that they took the group up near Mosul, to the ISIS-held territory. The aid workers who were going to be released are now being classified as hostages. We have two from Uganda, one from Sweden, and one from Bulgaria."

T.J. Talbot raised his hand and barked before being given permission. "When was this? And are we sure they aren't still on the road?"

"They were picked up by an Army personnel carrier, one of ours, by the way, a present to the Iraqi forces upon our departure, except it got captured or sold to ISIS. They traveled along with supplies for their training camp, which we think is here." Kyle pointed to a red X slightly south of Mosul. "Although not spotted, we believe they made it up there in five hours due to road conditions. We have satellite images to thank for that. Unfortunately, most APCs look alike and from the sky don't tell us who is in them or in what condition."

This was an area the SEALs had known well, since earlier operations involving snatch and grabs were conducted in nearby villages before the SEALs were tasked to train Iraqi forces who would turn so they would later become their opposition in the killing fields. It was never lost on any of them that they had trained their adversaries to fight just like they did. And the US forces had generously left them great equipment to use as well. Some of the fighters were formidable, and they had an endless supply of willing recruits ready to die for their cause if they failed.

"We're going to drop in here. The Kurds will get us to the border, but we're not using any Iraqis except for your terp," Kyle pointed to a thin man who was dressed in camo, but without the tats and bulging arms he looked more like a shopkeeper.

Coop was on his feet so fast he literally bumped into T.J. who was rushing to the terp's side. "Jackie!"

Alex had never worked with this man before, but he knew the Iraqi interpreter had saved many of their lives over the tours his other teammates had gone on. His nickname was Jackie Daniels, his alias given him because it was easy to remember and didn't give the man's true identity. It was a huge asset to have him along, especially if they had to embed in a village or town and not be noticed.

Alex took his cue from Kyle, who watched the hasty reunion with little joy. He wondered if Kyle wasn't getting tired of seeing people he loved and respected placed in harm's way, especially for something that should not have happened. It was becoming a broken record these days. Missing machinery, parts, ammunition, people killed due to lack of preparation. Lives sacrificed while reaching for another weapon to help defend their brothers.

He saw in Kyle's face the wear and tear of the burden of planning, executing and bearing the brunt of the decisions, and then the burden of the explanations when things didn't go as planned.

Alex knew that although tired and nearly thirty-five years of age, having spent over fifteen years as a SEAL, Kyle would tell him, if he dared to ask, that it was the job he was made for. That gave Alex courage. Someday he'd transmit that courage to younger SEALs coming up the ranks. Take their testy asses and make men out of them. Men their mothers would love in life and honor in death if need be. It was a man's work to defend the innocent. At some point in the development of a hardened SEAL, the laughter and smack talk happened only to let off steam and not to be a hotshot. It was the way they kept the cobwebs that preceded Dr.

Death and his absurd zombie ambulance crew from claiming any of them.

The rest of the instructions went quick. He fist-bumped Ryan and Cory, who already looked up to him because he was chosen to put his life on the line, and they were chosen to be backup.

"You keep their focus here, okay? Something happens, you guys yell and scream and make sure we aren't cut off with our dicks hanging, hear?" He followed it up with a smile just so they didn't think he was really serious.

Except of course, he was.

OF ALL THE rides to the sandbox, this one was the worst. Maybe it was because he'd spent so much time smoothing and kissing Miss Sydney's silky skin, and listening to subtle changes in the way she breathed, in the way she talked to herself when she didn't think he was listening. He could see her standing on a beach in her skimpy bathing suit.

Damn, I've not seen that action. When he got back, he intended to have her show him all her best moves. He'd reward her with kisses anywhere she wanted and he'd make love to her in the sand if she wanted it bad enough. Made no difference to him. Even going shopping for fresh fruit, red meat, and wine would be an orgasmic experience for him. These were all things he now realized he had never had.

He'd fix that shit soon as he returned.

Mark was throwing up from the ride, heaving into a plastic bag. Coop let T.J. tend to him, finally giving him a shot for his nausea. Fredo was discussing child rearing with Coop. Alex knew damn well Coop could only hear every other word, and with Fredo's heavily accented Spanglish and "isms," his phobias for health food and anything green except chilies and cilantro, Coop was probably hearing a story or an opinion he'd heard already twice today. Fredo never seemed to catch on that he could be boring as hell. No one had the heart to tell him because of the size of his dedication to the Team.

Kyle was asleep, and Alex was glad for that.

He looked at all the faces of the men he served with, all of whom left someone special at home. All except Jake. Because Coop probably told Kyle about Sydney. The ones left behind were single. He wondered if that was intentional.

Damn right it is. There wasn't anything Kyle did that wasn't in a plan. But he also wondered why he sent the married or committed ones in and not the unattached. Maybe it had to do with the children, and what these men might be able to emotionally handle. Maybe he didn't want the ones who could detach from the sight of kids being abused.

They landed after dark in the northern border region with Turkey. A small band of Kurdish fighters checked them out carefully, making eye contact with each of them. The shared expression of resolve gave the mission a higher likelihood of success. It was always the same with them. Tough as nails, defending their land filled with refugees from all over, camping out in fields their grandfathers had farmed, sharing their cattle, their water, maybe their women, but fighting just the same to preserve what they were forced to share.

He liked these guys. They were smart. Worst thing about their situation was that they didn't have the pull with either the US or with Turkey, and certainly not with the Bagdad government. He'd spent an afternoon pawing through dead bodies after one especially bloody engagement with the enemy on his first deployment. No ammunition could be left behind for two reasons: it either could come back to get you or it would leave a good Kurdish fighter without the means to defend himself, or you.

After his first tour, that dream of checking pockets and vests, finding pictures of wives and babies amongst the dead enemy, looking for intel and ammunition, had kept him awake at night. It wasn't the sort of thing he could get rid of with a few beers or a woman who wanted to impress a SEAL with her own moves. He just had to wait it out until the bright memory faded into a gray fog.

When those visions stopped fading, that's when he knew he'd be done. Or when going to bed became something he dreaded because he couldn't do it any longer. If he needed pills, he was done.

They moved quietly in a convoy without lights. The mission had been planned for a full moon, and the stars were always bright in this region of the world because of the lack of big electric grids. Moonlight made the roadside look wet like they were jeeping it down for a midnight swim in San Diego. Only thing they couldn't see without their NV headsets were the whites of the animals who dared to live here despite the carnage. Mostly skinny dogs. The fighters told him at one time the land was plentiful with small animals.

The building they were to sleep in for a few hours was an abandoned school that contained a fallout shelter, of all things. Two Kurdish men had guarded the place so they didn't have to take up valuable time clearing the structure—except Kyle insisted they do so anyhow.

The yellow radioactive sticker was nearly removed from the latch cover to the shelter. Some enemy forces had been routed out six months ago, but not before they had created a tunnel system that went who knows where. Figuring that out was going to be their job, but not until the light of day came upon them. Right now, they had to settle, eat a little, and get some sleep, taking turns.

Jake handed him a piece of goat jerky he'd picked up at the village in Turkey. It was actually quite good.

"They make this for us, you know. They don't eat goat in that village, but they have a rather good cottage industry selling it to Special Forces coming through. Look how they spell Teriyaki."

Alex laughed at the "Terri Yaqi" label. "As long as it isn't poisoned."

"Nah. They said it was okay," he answered pointing to their transportation and guard team.

"Gives you terrible farts," Jackie added. "Careful or it will announce your approach."

Alex and Jake chuckled.

"So you have two little ones now, Jackie, right?"

"Yes, Mr. T.J. Trying to keep up with you. But see, I'm a smaller man. You are the virile American."

"Horseshit. Being tall has nothing to do with it. It's how healthy you eat," said Coop. Fredo scowled and turned to the wall, pretending to take a nap.

Danny was listening to the wind above them. Little pebbles were pinging on top of the metal roof of the school. "Sandstorm," he whispered. "And I smell rain."

"No shit?" Jake said. "You can smell rain?"

"Personally, I think it's donkey piss," said Jackie

with a grin.

Danny leaned into the three of them, "Do you know the worst place you can be during a lightning storm and flash flood?" he asked.

Alex knew what he was going to say before he actually did.

Jake was going to be the wiseguy. "On an all metal, fully-lit-up Ferris wheel?"

"Shush," Kyle whispered. "Get some rest because tomorrow's a big day."

Alex sat back. If it was ten hours' difference, then it would be close to noon at home. He'd be lounging by the pool, trying to coax that suit off Sydney, and making her dance for him on the diving board. And then he'd let her dance on his lap and send him to Heaven.

CHAPTER 19

B EFORE LEAVING FOR San Diego, Sydney previewed an apartment in a new complex on the north side of Santa Rosa, not too far from the gym and close to the freeway. With the move-in bonuses, she only had to leave a $100 deposit. Subject to her credit, which she knew was excellent, the attractive two-bedroom place on the top floor was hers. The large balcony off the living room faced east, but wrapped around three sides of the apartment. It would be perfect for having morning coffee or breakfast after an early morning run or workout.

She dictated notes for all the details she had to handle when she got back to town. By the time she got to her place and connected her computer to the Internet, the list would be transcribed and waiting for her. Next, she dialed her roommate.

"Okay, Sydney. As usual, your timing's perfect. I'm moving to Florida."

"Seriously?"

"Got a coaching job there."

"Awesome."

"Was just going to stay here for the summer to not leave you in the lurch, but since you already did that—"

"Oh, come on. I would have helped you pay for it, if I left you stuck with the full rent."

"I know. I'm just jealous. Things are really looking up for you. And there's a new man in your life. About time."

Before Sydney could respond, her roommate interrupted. "Oh gosh, Jack said to give him a call. He's been a pest."

"I'll bet."

"Says he's been trying to get in contact with you for several days."

"He knew exactly where I was, and I've only been gone four days total." Sydney checked her phone, which was on vibrate and sure enough, there were several messages from Jack. And one voice message. "Okay. I see them. I'll call him next."

She stopped by her landlord's real estate office and told her about the move. There was always a waiting list for little houses down by the beach. Moving out quickly wasn't a problem because the rent always went up for the next person in line.

So that left Jack. At first she got the sound of his

message recording. "Okay, Jack, sorry I didn't call you back—"

"Sydney! You're back. You were going to let me know."

"I told you where I was going. Sorry, I forgot to call." Her stomach lurched with what she had to tell him next. "Um, Jack, things have made a dramatic shift for me. I'm excited to tell you I've chosen a partner to train with, but it will mean I move up to Sonoma County."

"Really? Wow. I thought—"

"I know. This is sudden for me too, but I really like the direction everything is headed. So I'm going to withdraw from the co-ed league. I hope you can find a replacement for the tournament coming up. Maybe Holly?"

"Stop it, Sydney. Now you're making fun of me."

Only Jack would take a photograph of himself and think it was a cartoon. "I think my plan is going to work. And I like the idea of training in some degree of privacy."

"How are you going to get to games?"

"Well, it's not like we'll be in the middle of Africa. They do have cable and satellite here. And we won't be ready for qualifiers for several months, maybe a year."

"Of course. Dumb question."

"So, I'm afraid this is it. Hopefully, in about a year

you'll see me at the beach events with Carly."

"Okay, kid. You'll be the one that got away."

"Aw, Jack. The way I see it, maybe you'll stay married longer this time."

"Ouch." After a brief silence. "Okay, best of luck, Sydney."

BACK AT HER bungalow, she removed her trophies, plaques, and her pictures, some of them taken in high school. She saw one with the Golden Gate Bridge in the background as she stood with her dad when he was healthy. She touched his image with her forefinger as if she could make the connection again.

Her resentment towards her mother for having forced her father to leave their home hadn't waned. With her mother's radical mood swings and wild ideas and boyfriends, Sydney had become the parent and her mother the child. The woman wasn't capable of taking care of anyone, including herself, and went from loser to loser, each "friend" a little scarier than the last. Finally, Sydney'd had enough and reached out to her father, who welcomed her with open arms. He put braces on her teeth, spent hours helping her with homework and bumping the ball around the yard. She had never felt so safe or so loved.

She packed the photographs and picture albums with the trophies. Under the blotter on her desk was the funeral notice for her father's service. She'd forgotten she'd saved it there.

After her father died, they had to wait three days until they could find her mom, who had been partying in Las Vegas with future ex-husband number five or six. Sydney was grateful she and her dad had talked about her future and his finances. He left a sizeable trust fund administered by an attorney friend of his. It had been the first thing her mother inquired about, and it didn't surprise Sydney one bit.

She read over the Order of Service, and the thank you from the family, and then discovered the message she'd written just for him:

"You were the best dad a girl could ever want. These past two years with you have been the best I'll probably ever have. I'm not sure how I'll get over missing you, but I know for sure I'll never stop loving you. I will make you proud, Dad. Your Favorite Giraffe."

She'd forgotten he used to buy her stuffed giraffes. All arms and legs with practically no meat on her, she fit the description of his favorite nickname for her.

The notice was tucked carefully between two glass-framed awards, the awards added to a box, and one by one, all the boxes were stacked in the living room.

The next morning, moving men came, loading

boxes, various pieces of furniture including her bed, desk, the dining table, and her big screen TV. Into her Murano she placed a few of her valuables, her favorite pillow and comforter, and some other personal items for the return trip to Sonoma County. She said good-bye to the movers, who would keep her things in storage for a week until she made it back up to Santa Rosa and called for them.

When she moved to San Diego two years ago, the first thing she did was sit on the deck at the Hotel Del Coronado and have chowder and a margarita over-looking the ocean, then walk down the beach and watch the young men in their boat crews trying to pass this little segment of the grueling BUD/S course required before they could move on to SEAL Qualification Training. Her friends had told her about this special breed of men, one in a thousand regular Navy ever getting to apply. And the pass rate for any of them to become full-fledged Navy SEALs could vary from 5 percent to maybe 20 percent by the time all was said and done.

So this being her last day in San Diego for a time, she decided to do the same again. The restaurant was packed since it was near the weekend. Outside, she had to share a section surrounding an unlit fire pit with several couples of various ages, celebrating birthdays or anniversaries. Though she felt out of place, she hoped someday to be one of those couples.

She finished her chowder and her drink, but picked up her French bread and took the wooden steps down to the white sand. She could barely see orange netting separating the beach from the training area. As she got closer, there was a crowd of people taking pictures, sitting and watching the men pick up the little rubber boats, put them on their heads in teams of ten or twelve, and navigate them over a rocky barrier that was sharp, craggy, and slippery. The boat was never allowed to touch the rocks or it had to be brought back to starting position. Once the rocks were scaled, the boat was put into the water.

Some of the boats capsized, dumping everyone out into the surf. Other teams drifted right out through the whitewater and into the inlet area, waiting for permission to come ashore. The same drill was done over and over again. Teams were yelled at by instructors with bullhorns. Two recruits were doing sit-ups in the surf for some sort of infraction. One boat crew was allowed a rare moment of rest, sitting at the edges of their rubber boat, oars pointed to the sky, watching all the activity before them. They cheered encouragement and shouted warnings to their fellow Team members. Other teams that groaned or occasionally complained were rewarded with a wet and sandy. Another team with several men who laughed as they ran by their fellow recruits' bad luck were ordered to join them in the surf.

The first day here and now the last day, she paid homage to these brave young men. With any luck perhaps one would permanently become a part of her life.

She blew the young men a kiss, turned on her heel, and headed back to the parking lot and then to the highway leading north.

THE APARTMENT WAS just as lovely as she'd remembered it. With no bed or furniture, she wrapped herself in her comforter, took a water bottle out on the balcony, and sat gazing at the red glow of the sunset. Tomorrow she and Carly would have their first real training day. She'd found her old workout schedule from college to use as a guide.

She closed her eyes and wondered what Alex was doing.

Be safe, my love. Come back to me.

CHAPTER 20

KYLE ASKED ALEX and Danny to accompany him on a scouting mission to see if they could locate the missing children. He'd had limited contact with the drone handler and not much had been learned, except the armored personnel carrier hadn't moved from the large hall adjacent to a bombed-out factory of some kind. Thinking it might be left there for a quick escape, they decided that's where they'd check first. They were mic'ed up. Cooper and Fredo were to listen in and comment if necessary from their bunker.

The Kurdish fighters struck up a conversation with Jackie in a pigeon Pashtu common to all of them. Jackie addressed Kyle.

"They say they've heard noises, perhaps an injured dog or something. They are not sure." Jackie shrugged.

"Maybe one of the kids?" asked Danny.

"My bet would be one of the aid workers," answered Kyle. "Those animals won't let them alone, and maybe that's a good thing in disguise. Gives the kids a fighting chance if the guards are preoccupied."

Jackie began the guttural singsong conversation again and then nodded. "They have not seen any women here for some time. And they do not know the exact number of guards."

Alex thought that whatever was going on in there, if this was the right place, it was fully self-contained, and he commented so. Kyle nodded.

"Ask them when their supplies come in, and if they ever leave to do a perimeter search or take a leak," demanded Kyle.

Jackie gave them the answer. "No leaks, no one comes and goes. But they are fastidious about taking out the trash. They leave white garbage bags outside the door first thing in the morning. A truck comes by once a day to pick up all the trash."

"So we steal one of those bags. That will tell us what is going on inside," said Kyle.

"I should go with you, Kyle," whispered Jackie.

"We're not here to talk, my friend. I need you to listen on the com in case we're overrun." He ordered Fredo to give him a mic. "You're more helpful telling me what I'm hearing, okay?"

"Okay, boss."

"Armando, you be ready. T.J., you help Fredo get out some flashy stuff we might need. See if there is anything here you guys can use."

"Roger that, Kyle. Do I have permission to move around outside?" answered T.J.

"Not yet. I can't take the chance someone saw us come in and is waiting in the wings to pick us off one at a time or radio for help. Stay invisible."

The town was without power either day or night, but at night the SEALs had the aid of specialized equipment. It gave them two very good reasons to explore then: it was cooler and it was easier for them to maneuver undetected.

There was one gas station operating with a generator attached to one pumping station. Dogs barked in the distance as they drew nearer to the building.

The roar of an oncoming jeep or large truck had them ducking into a doorway of a bombed home. The truck continued on its route without stopping at the warehouse building. Alex heard relief in the sighs of the men.

They kept to the shadows. There were lots of partial walls and piles of debris. Of biggest concern were explosive devices either left on purpose or left behind by retreating troops of either side. A no-man's land that technically was controlled by ISIS, there was no way to tell what fortification or level of manpower they'd encounter up ahead. The drones wouldn't be out until dawn, and they didn't have the intel on the ground that SEALs had used in the past. Their heat monitors showed nothing but small animal signatures, but the bright moon was interfering with the map.

A pinkish glow had just formed on the horizon, and at first Alex thought there was a fire up ahead. It turned out to be the toxic sunrise generated from burning oil fields. A measured sniff confirmed that detail. They'd have to be quick about getting back or lose the element of surprise.

The thick walls of the warehouse were not yielding anything from their new Graphene Sensors. Alex wondered if the bad guys had gotten smart about not positioning anyone inside against the perimeter walls.

One by one they hugged the perimeter and still no heat signature. Of concern was the fact that there were no windows or doors except the one in front facing the street. Alex guessed the enemy had selected this building carefully, knowing a rescue operation might ensue. This would be easier to defend or to control the outcome on the insides if compromised. Though this forward planning was disturbing, he'd been trained to read the enemy's intent and use whatever assumptions they had against them. Heavily laid plans were easiest to thwart with the element of surprise.

He guessed Kyle would create a breach of the walls of the building rather than attempt to use the entrance where they'd be expected.

Kyle was relaying intel back to the camp when they heard voices and someone coughing, coming from inside. And then they heard the distinct whimper of someone in pain, unable to control it. It did sound like an animal, like a dog. But it could also be a child.

Danny's jaw was set, and he closed his eyes, focusing on the noise. Someone was whispering a word they couldn't understand.

"You hear that?" asked Kyle.

"No, sir," came Coop's response.

"Sounds like *motley*, something like that," Kyle answered. Danny and Alex nodded in agreement. "See if you can get a translation. Jackie?"

"No, boss. I've never heard that language."

"So get some help. Coop? Swedish? Bulgarian? Ugandan?"

"Swahili, sir."

"What does it mean?"

"I'm just saying it would be Swahili, not Ugandan."

The coughing continued, followed by another moan, *"Mauti."* Muffled voices and more coughing ensued from multiple sources. Danny opened his eyes at the sounds, which brightened his countenance. It appeared the coughing was intentionally done to hide the sounds of the injured party's moans.

"I'm confirming multiple persons, and I'm going to say they do sound like women or children. More than a handful," Kyle said to his earpiece.

"Roger that. Will relay," said Coop. "Working on *motley* too."

Kyle motioned toward another old storefront with the roof caved in, missing all its windows. It was located at the rear of the subject building, but still gave them a vantage of the street. The APC gave them partial cover, but blocked their view of oncoming traffic under the carriage or around the body of the APC.

The sky began to turn lighter gray with a pink tinge to it.

"We're coming back in five." Kyle pointed to his eyes, asking Danny and Alex to search for something they could use. Danny came up with some strips of cloth and a leather belt. Alex found two metal tins opened by a key, covered in what appeared to be Russian writing. The rolled edge was sharp enough to cut through a thick hide. A couple of cardboard boxes looked familiar, and they were surprised to find a board game of some kind using colored marbles. Danny was ecstatic with his find and filled two pockets with the little glass orbs.

They slipped down the back alleyway, again hugging the shadows of buildings, stopping to check out if anyone had eyes on them.

They heard the distinctive metal sound of a latch

being pulled back and a door on creaky hinges being opened.

A small figure with a mop of dark hair held a plastic garbage bag, depositing it in the street, just before a hand yanked him backward and shut the metal door. The boy's anguished yell drilled fear down Alex' spine, but Danny was grinning from ear to ear.

"I swear that's Ali. He's alive, guys. We're gonna get him," said an animated Danny.

"Hold that thought. We got a bunch of incoming. You guys make yourselves invisible and hope to God they're just moving through," said Coop.

The trio quickly ducked into another hovel of some kind. They could still smell food, as if someone had lived there recently. A makeshift mattress in the corner, made up of rags and old hides appeared to have been someone's bed for a time.

Soon, four large Russian military trucks drove through the dusty downtown area, turned right and then proceeded without stopping.

"I'm gonna get that bag," said Danny.

"No wait." Kyle directed his next comment to Coop. "Anything more?"

"I think we're clear for now."

Kyle nodded. Without making a sound, the Navajo SEAL ran with lightning speed, picked up the white garbage bag, tucked it under his jacket and returned without breaking a sweat.

"Good work. We're coming back, with a package," whispered Kyle.

CHAPTER 21

SYDNEY WENT FOR a five-mile run before she got to the gym and still was nearly twenty minutes early. The bookkeeper, Mrs. Beeson, let her in and signed a key to her name. The heavyset black woman waddled in shoes that squeaked as she showed Sydney where her personal locker was and where the equipment and supplies were stored.

"Don't you worry none about your first day. They might have you work the café just so you get to meet the girls. In time, you'll get to know the coaches and the mothers who practically live here. But I'm gonna let Ruthie figure it out for you, so you just sit tight and wait for Carly, okay?

Sydney liked her kind eyes and gentle demeanor.

"Can I help you with something, Mrs. Beeson?"

"Oh lord, child. I gotta concentrate on that new payroll system they purchased. I don't get those checks out, and you know what'll happen. You just don't worry that pretty little head of yours."

On the way back to the sand courts the woman turned to her. "How'd you get to be so tall?"

"Genetics. Can't be the food or the water. I grew up in Southern California."

"My son Mason was a tall boy. If he was still around, I'd be trying to fix the two of you together," the woman said.

"Well, in my case, I have a boyfriend, so it wouldn't work. Maybe Carly though."

"No, I'm sorry, the Lord saw fit to take my Mason overseas. That's not anything a mother should ever have to get over. He was a good boy." She walked to her desk, picked up a small school photograph and handed it to Sydney. She stared down at the picture of a handsome young man in a maroon graduation cap and gown.

It took all the effort she had to hand the picture back to Mrs. Beeson and thank her. Mrs. Beeson was talking on and on about how he'd enlisted right out of high school, would have played football in college, but he wanted to serve his country.

"Shouldn't have happened to a war hero. Did I tell you he was a hero?"

Sydney's hand was shaking. She needed water, and she couldn't get air all of a sudden.

"Excuse me, I have to go to the ladies room," she

said and dashed down the hallway. She sat on the closed lid of the toilet and put her head in her hands. Recognizing she was having a panic attack, she wet down a paper towel and placed it at the back of her neck, sat back down and waited until the coolness settled her nerves.

When she heard Carly's voice, she stood, splashed water on her face, blotted it dry with her tank top, washed her hands again, and dashed out into the hallway to meet her new partner.

They shook hands. "They say all partnerships are never as good as your first working day together," Sydney said. "So, welcome to our first and perhaps our best." She was forcing her smile but found it worked.

Carly chuckled. "Yup, the new car or boat effect. You're absolutely in love with it that day. Only later do you find all the flaws you'd forgotten to think about or discounted as not being important enough."

They started taking turns setting and bumping while they talked casually. "You get a run in earlier?" Carly asked.

"Sure did."

"You tell me when I can pick it up," Carly said.

"Any time, bitch."

They played opposites and lobbed the ball back and forth over the net, angling it just enough so that the other person had to really stretch to keep from letting the ball hit the ground. After they got to the count of one hundred, Sydney picked up the pace. First she served, hitting the ball as hard as she could, nearly getting an ace every time. Carly didn't show her any mercy and did the same for another twenty five serves against Sydney. It didn't take long before Sydney wished she'd worn her suit, not the spandex and sports bra. She was covered in sweat and had downed half a gallon of water already. She only drank lots of water during trainings, never during a tournament until the play was over.

Two freshman players from Sonoma State approached after Carly waived them over. The four of them played hard, alternating partners, until at last Carly and Sydney worked together, which was a combination that was practically impossible for the new girls to defend against.

Sydney began to feel the rhythm of what their play would be like.

Over lunch, she talked about her workout from her college days.

"I knew you were a beach player. Now I wish I'd come to watch you before," said Carly.

"One of my teammates showed me the beach scene one summer. And man, I was hooked. But the scholarship was for indoor team play. And, as you know, when they're paying for you to go to college, they own you."

"It's a job."

"It is." Sydney dried her face off with a white fluffy towel. She pulled out her workout folder and the notebook she used to track her daily events, sharing how she alternated between doing heavy cardio and weight training, going lean and then binging. How she set up focus work such as serving, digging, and working on her foot speed with the ladder and the vertical leap trainer.

"We don't have those. Sort of a liability for the gym," Carly said pointing to the devices.

"I get it. I'll order them, okay? Not sure about the jumper, but I'm sure the ladder I can carry around in my trunk. If we go out to the coast, I'll have it. Make a training day out of a nice drive."

"Perfect! I'm going to modify this for me, too. This is excellent, Sydney."

After their lunch break, they worked side by side serving, then practiced roofing each other by working at the net. In regular team play, most opponents were ready for Sydney's killer spikes, and she'd been known in high school for breaking a good number of nose cartilages. She'd developed a quick swish move at the net so that instead of drilling the ball, she lobbed it carefully to a strategic place that was nearly impossible for Carly to reach.

They took a water break later on, and she watched the high school players parade in again like yesterday.

"It's an after-school league. Works because they get to play on a team with players whom they normally are competing against."

It made sense. *You always improve faster playing against an opponent who is better than you are.*

She watched them giggle, fix their ribbons and adjust their knee pads. They talked about sparkly nail polish and where they were going to go on vacation. Sydney watched the young players as if they were some alien species. She never had parents on the bleachers cheering her on during her last high school days.

She moved back in with her mother after her father passed. Her mother began leaving for several days at a time, which was a blessing. Sydney drove herself around to practices in her father's old BMW and agreed to pay rent as long as her mother never brought her boyfriends home. Her father's money paid for coaching and memberships on traveling teams, as well as recruiting trips. By the time she was a junior in high school, she was maintaining a heavy traveling schedule and was being sought after by several colleges Though she still lived at home, she was pretty much on her own. Graduation came and went. Her mother was a no show, and Sydney celebrated with the family of one of her teammates. She couldn't wait to get out of town and get to college, to have that life of her own. Her college scholarship was her way out of Dodge.

She studied the kids and their doting parents. It was even worse than down south. The spoiled little girls gave nasty looks to their mothers when they didn't care for the way their hair had turned out. They left half-finished sandwiches and tossed bottles of water after a couple of sips.

They have no idea what they're throwing away.

BEFORE SHE LEFT that day, Sydney made a copy of her workout plan for Carly, and they agreed to meet again in the morning for a run first. "Tomorrow you start being useful here. I'm going to give you a boy's team that comes in on Sunday mornings. They're a lot of fun. In the afternoon, you'll do your first birthday party, but I'll be there to help."

"Cool."

THE TALK ABOUT going to the beach made her think of this part of California's coast. She put the top down and drove the half hour to watch the rough surf crash down on the beach, which was more rock than sand. A couple of surfers in wet suits braved the cold waters of the Pacific, ever mindful of sharks and sinkholes in the dangerous Northern Californian coastline.

It was a different scene than the one she'd been at

in San Diego. Less crowded and way colder with a brisk wind pulling fog behind it. She knew she would sleep well tonight having inhaled her fill of this fresh ocean breeze. Since nearly everything she did today was a new routine, her systems were overloaded. It had been years since she'd felt so relaxed.

Though it had gotten chilly she kept her top down and turned on the heated seats, playing some satellite country music she could sing along to. The hills were beginning to turn golden brown the further away from the ocean she got. Unlike other parts of the country, the biggest changes in colors occurred between the green of spring and the golden yellow-brown of summer. Dairy cows grazed and occasionally got onto the roadway, causing her to veer. She could see herself living here year-round. She planned on finding out what Sonoma County had to offer.

And then of course there was Alex. What would he want for her? She wondered what he was doing right now, if he was allowing the sights of a strange sunrise in a foreign land make him miss her. She hoped so. She hoped he was finding answers to what they were searching for. Hoped there was some important mission being executed flawlessly.

Come back to me soon, Alex.

CHAPTER 22

D ANNY DROPPED THE plastic bag in the middle of their little circle. The two Kurds looked at each other and then turned down their lips in disgust as Cooper carefully undid the twist tie, just like in any kitchen at home. Coop held up the red fastener band with tiny metal wire threaded through it.

"Glad bag."

Alex nearly lost it. If the citizens of the US could see them now, huddling over a garbage bag in the night, in a dirty cave with no heat, in the middle of the killing lands between two opposing armies, they would question the millions of dollars spent training them all. They might even ask for a refund.

"I'm going to examine the patient very carefully," Coop said as he placed a facemask over his mouth like he was about to operate. Holding his gloved hands in the air, twirling his fingers he added, "The patient has but one orifice and I'm going in to explore now." He frowned, opened wide the plastic bag and stuck his head inside.

Team members were darting worried glances all around until Coop abruptly pulled his sandy brown pelt of a scalp up. In his best Dr. Frankenstein imitation he held between his thumb and forefinger a small, odd-looking, one-inch-long bug, it's bulbous body and crablike legs wiggling, trying to get loose. "It's alive! It's alive!" Coop said in a sinister whisper.

The Kurds whispered urgently in their own tongue, and Jackie laughed, pointing out Coop's find, "They lay their eggs in the bellies of dead camels. So, they are called camel spiders," he said, barely able to maintain.

"I understand they are quite good roasted," Coop said, his eyes still wild. Jackie nearly fell over backward laughing. The Kurds distanced themselves even further.

"You sure that bug didn't bite you?" asked Kyle.

"Gimme that thing," said Fredo, who yanked the insect from Coop's claws and burned it alive with a cigarette lighter. He tossed the still flaming carcass to the side. "Problem solved."

"They are harmless, my friend," Jackie said with a grin.

Fredo picked up what was left of the bug, squeezed the body and a green puss-like fluid came out. "This shit?" he said as he pointed to it. "You get this shit on your skin, and it will itch for five, count them, five days, comrades."

"Did not know that," said Kyle, very matter of fact. Armando and Danny were punching each other, hiding their chuckles behind their gloved hands.

T.J. was always the adventurous one. "Where'd you learn that, Frodo?"

"In an outhouse." Fredo's defiant stare gave way to his need to share. "I sat on one, that's how I know."

There were snickers all around the tunnel. Alex was streaming tears.

One of the Kurd fighters tapped an earpiece and said a word to Jackie.

"Listen up!" Jackie whispered. "They say a single truck is about three klicks out, heading this way."

Coop dove back into the bag and the horseplay stopped. He peeled back the plastic so everyone could aid in the search. They found several plastic fruit juice containers and straws. He nodded as he held up a bloody woman's sanitary napkin. "This is why the trash has to be taken out every day."

"So one of the aid workers is alive," whispered Alex.

"Or one of the children is of age," said Jackie. "They consider puberty to be at nine years, my friends."

But what Coop found next disturbed them all.

There were bloody bandages made from strips of torn cloth. The discharge on the cloth was a light brownish yellow, mixed with blood.

"Someone's got a helluva infection. I'm not seeing any evidence of antibiotic creams, and I sure as hell don't think that person's on oral meds," Coop said after he sniffed the rags.

They quickly went through every piece of trash, saving cups, straws or anything that could aid in DNA identification if it came to that. Coop snipped off one section of bloody bandage and placed it in a plastic sandwich container. They found unfiltered cigarette butts, which could also be useful in identification since it was unlikely the children or the aid workers smoked.

At the very bottom, placed in another plastic bag, were pieces of magazine pages used as toilet paper.

He quickly returned the contents to the plastic Glad bag, refastened the twist tie, and handed the bag to Kyle. Danny grabbed it and departed their sanctuary.

"Alex and Armando, you watch him. Armani watch them tight."

Headlights flooded the abandoned buildings three houses down, and then flooded the roadway in front of their bunker with light. Armando trained his 300 Win on the driver, following the path the enemy's head traveled until they heard the squeal of brakes and a grinding of gears. The truck lurched, sputtered, and died halfway between their lookout and the entrance to the building housing the children.

In the moonlight, the white garbage bag shone like a giant free-formed pumpkin. Alex couldn't see Danny anywhere. The driver got out, walked to the doorway, picked up the bag, walked the short distance back to the truck and hoisted the bag into the back. With a backfire, he started the truck back up, nearly flooding it and was on his way into the town center via the winding descent.

Armando dropped the scope, surveying the horizon, which was now getting light bluish gray. All at once, Danny was right there in front of them. Alex felt like he'd jumped ten feet.

"Whoa. I didn't hear a thing. One minute I was looking out there and the next, boom, you were there," said Alex.

"That's kind of the point," returned Danny.

Aware they were not entirely invisible, the three team guys retreated to the safety of the underground bunker.

Kyle was on the phone with the Headshed discussing their options. Though they had heard someone complaining, the lives of the children didn't look in imminent danger, but that could change at any time.

"They're going to get a heat-seeking drone. We've

ordered three birds since I'm hoping we can get everybody. We confirmed an injury, someone in pain who might be the same person, and a relatively healthy and brave little boy," Kyle's voice wobbled. "We go at oh-one-hundred, which means we rest up now and into the heat of the day. If we're not disturbed, we find another spot for tomorrow if we're still here, since the shed thinks it's likely our drop was spotted."

Alex listened while peeling off his vest and unbuttoning his shirt to get rid of the restriction he felt about his middle and get fresh air. He needed to drift off into a deep sleep quickly. Maybe it would all be over in twenty-four hours, and he'd be on his way home. He saw green fields waving in the breeze and vineyards stretched across hills in tight, perfect rows.

Kyle's words were droning on and on until at last they were coming from Sydney's lips and Alex was back in her bedroom as she rubbed against him and whispered battle plans.

HE AWOKE TO the smell of baby wipes. Danny had already been out and stolen a bag of oranges he'd found in a home recently bombed. The delicious fruit was literally inhaled by the group after they washed their faces and hands with the wipes.

Alex alternated with some bits of the dried goat jerky. Jackie passed around some glorious jasmine rice he'd brought from home. With bottled water that almost tasted sweet it was so pure, he was well satisfied in minutes and ready to start his new day at nearly midnight.

Kyle had good news about the extraction. Based on movements that had been tracked by satellite, it was determined the ISIS leaders had been planning an offensive on the north side of town beyond the town center. So the concentration of manpower was some five or six klicks away, which gave them a decent window to do a full-on raid.

Weapons checked and rechecked, each man had the laundry list of personal things they brought into battle. Their Invisios were adjusted and synched so their command could hear the chatter. Alex watched Danny stow a small red slingshot matching the larger one he'd been practicing with earlier and knew it was for little Ali.

They marked time and left the safety of their compound.

Fredo and Danny set charges along the back wall of the building. T.J. and Rory would cover the street, with Coop, Lucas and Mark going in behind the front door when it was breached. Armando and Jake took their perches on top of two abandoned buildings. That left Alex to attend to the breach of the back wall with Kyle. Danny would handle any problems with entry in case more explosives were required and then would accompany them. Jackie would follow behind. Fredo would man the alleyway behind and take care of escapees or signal any reinforcements coming to the aid of the guards inside.

The timed devices went off exactly as planned. The building construction was so weak, half the roof collapsed in the rear, so instead of crawling through a neat square hole, they had to navigate over rubble and falling debris from on top. The front door had been loaded with charges from the inside as well, so most the front of the building had collapsed, T.J. reported. Immediately Alex heard automatic weapons from the front of the building, which meant someone was on sentry detail.

The interior was thick with smoke but his night vision goggles clicked in after the initial blasts, and interior walls and doorways began to form. He heard children screaming and the staccato commands of guards who were scrambling for their weapons.

He and Danny found the children huddled in one corner of the room with two women standing defiantly in front of them to protect them.

"We're from the United States of America, and we're here to get you out." Danny's voice hung in the room like thick smoke. Through the wall of children out came Ali, who ran straight for the big SEAL.

Danny kneeled to accept the hug of the little boy. "We're bringing you home," he said over Ali's head.

Alex guarded the doorway, hearing spotty gunfire and the ever-present "clear" as each room was searched and neutralized. He turned, counted ten children and three adults, and gave the count to Kyle and the others.

"And looks like Danny has Ali."

"Anyone injured?" Kyle's question was answered all around in the negative.

"Kids appear okay," said Danny.

Jackie raced inside the room and spoke with the aid workers, who did not speak Pashtu. "Swedish. I need to go to language school in Monterey, learn some Swedish. My Russian is so poor, the Bulgarian girl cannot understand me," he said as he shrugged.

"You're all right, Jackie. We like you just the way you are," Alex reassured him.

Alex asked the workers in English and crude sign language where the fourth was located and they pointed to a litter in the corner covered with a bloody rag.

"Hold it, we got injured or worse, one of the workers. I'm checking now," Alex said. He pulled back the sheet and found the chalky face of one of the Ugandan workers and checked for vital signs finding none. "One worker dead." He recognized the bandages from the garbage bag. She'd suffered a large gash to her lower leg, hugely infected and still swollen at the time of her death. Her body wasn't yet stiff so the death had occurred within the past few hours.

"Hey, Danny and Jackie, we gotta be ready to move out," Alex reminded his teammate who was hugging the children and giving them water and small granola bar rations. Jackie was explaining to the children they would be going on a helicopter ride soon. That news was met with much enthusiasm.

Kyle appeared from down the hall. "We're all clear, Alex. Let's get these kids out the back."

"None of them have shoes. We're gonna have to carry them," he told his LPO.

"Okay, hear that? Everyone who isn't gathering intel, we need help with the hostages."

One by one the children and three remaining workers were carried over the rubble of the back wall, herded together and led on foot back toward their bunker. The familiar *whosh, whosh, whosh* of the birds was music to Alex' ears.

A box of cell phones and some maps were recovered. An old computer was also taken, but looked like it hadn't been used in months. As Alex left with one of the girls, he glanced back, stopping to watch Coop and T.J. gathering blood samples from the four KIAs. One of them appeared to be a boy of around ten years of age. T.J. was swearing profusely.

"Looks just like this kid," Coop whispered, pointing to a teen who lay dead beside him. Everyone scrambled with their precious cargo, some holding two kids, and exited what was left of the crumbling building within seconds.

Mark ran back to gather their duty bags left in the bunker and to sign off with the Kurdish fighters.

Everyone was safely loaded. Ali was in Danny's lap and clung to him with all the energy he could muster. Alex heard Danny reassure him he was taking him home. "California, Ali. You're going to California."

Alex watched the faces of the other children, some girls but mostly boys and all below the age of nine or ten, when they heard the word California. He could see there was hope that those plans might include them as well. Alex wished he could take them all, wished he could forever protect them from the horrors they must have witnessed in a war that was already underway the day they were born.

As they lifted off Armando clung to his perch in the doorway of one of the other Black Hawks while Alex guarded his. They could see a line of lights as a small convoy was heading toward the building they'd just liberated. He was surprised to see the air clear of counterattack measures from the ground.

As they ascended further and headed north to Turkish air space, Alex pulled back to take his seat amongst several of the children, one worker and two SEALs. Mark was chattering. Everyone was elated the mission had gone off without a casualty. Before long, two little girls were wrapped around his upper torso, crying into his uniform. He murmured unfamiliar words to the tops of their heads he knew they fully understood though they spoke no English.

"You shoulda seen those Kurds, man," Mark began. "I got the bags, I thanked them, called them brother, we high-fived it, and they just walked into the countryside and disappeared into thin air. No one was coming for them, they just walked out. I'm telling you, those guys are tough."

Alex wondered what was going through their minds when they saw the Americans and the hostages being flown to safety, if there was such a place in the region. But he understood the fight was on their turf and they had innocents of their own they needed to go home to and protect. The mission was over, but the war continued and probably would for many years to come.

Alex began to relax as he leaned against the seat and allowed himself to breathe in fresh mechanical-scented air.

I'm going home.

CHAPTER 23

S YDNEY GOT THE call she'd been hoping for.

"I'm back on US soil."

"Oh, so wonderful to hear your voice, Alex. Did everything work out?"

"Yup, about as good as it could have."

"Where were you exactly?"

"Sorry, sweetheart, no details over the phone. And I have to run, but wanted you to know I'm safely back."

"Thanks. I'm so relieved. So when will I see you again?"

"Not for a while. We have debriefing to do and interviews, like exit interviews. I'm going to be tied up for at least two weeks before I can get back there. It would be the same if you came down here, too."

Sydney was disappointed, but she knew it came with the territory. "I got it. Well, call when we can chat a bit. I'll let you go, then."

After another brief good-bye, they hung up.

He had not asked her how things had been going on her end. The call, after such a dangerous separation, was all too brief. She knew she should reel in her emotions and deal with the reality that it would always be a tug of war of priorities, but because of the nature of what he did, his life and career would most likely come first. She had never had this type of relationship with a man before, since Sydney was usually the one in control. She wondered as the weeks went by how this would settle with her.

Missing her dad was the most painful part of growing up. Maybe that's why she had such a tough exterior to most guys. Maybe that's why she tried so hard in everything she did. Was she making up for something she'd lost and would never find again? A man who unconditionally loved her, like her father? Or an adult relationship with someone who wouldn't abandon her like her mother?

She attributed her thoughts on these matters to a lack of focus and vowed to pound it out of herself. Over the next few days, she threw herself into the new job and her training with Carly. Some evenings they'd sit at her apartment and watch matches of the AVP qualifying tour. They caught up on gossip about the players they both knew.

Her conversations with Alex were the highlights of her week. Although awkward not being able to talk about his work, she told him what she was doing and he encouraged her.

"You find little things to focus on, make up stories in your head when it seems you're at an impasse. You remind yourself you can do way more than you thought," he said one day.

"Don't you have doubts?"

"Every day. But I trust the training. I trust the men I work with."

"Okay, I get that. You assume you have the skills, you just work to apply them."

"Exactly," Alex answered. "I'll bet you're way too hard on yourself. The only times I doubt are when I think of all the things that could go wrong. That's not a place I go. If I feel that way, then I haven't trained enough. Train for every eventuality."

Though she would have preferred to speak about other things, the fact that he was talking about something he was passionate about, gave her some hope. He wasn't keeping everything to himself.

"I agree, Alex. Everyone is always looking for the most talented athletes. What they sometimes overlook is their dedication to their training. You've heard the stories too, about future Hall of Fame athletes who got beat out on school teams because others were better players. But when those players didn't practice or hone their skills, they were passed over in favor of the athlete who would train so hard he'd become great."

"Yup. You got it."

"Someone wrote a book about talent being overrated."

"Everyone wants the short cut. Only the few greats are willing to dedicate themselves to their work." The awkward silence lingered until he broke it. "By the way, speaking of being prepared, I meant to tell you that several months ago we had an altercation with a home-grown terrorist cell up there in Cloverdale. We think they got rooted out, but stay safe. Keep your eyes and ears open always."

Sydney had never heard about this and decided she'd ask Carly tonight.

Hanging up was one of the hardest things she had to do, and she couldn't wait to see him again. He was still postponing coming up to visit, blaming it on his change in work situation, which annoyed her. And though logically she couldn't put her finger on it, she was feeling him distancing himself from her with each phone call. They needed time alone together again. The loss of the intensity between them was beginning to sting, but she tried not to let it show in her conversations.

She was put in charge of working with some of the younger, inexperienced coaches. Sydney discovered she was good negotiating with parents. Playing time was always a sensitive subject. Many of the young coaches who worked with teams at Beach had difficulty expressing themselves or speaking with authority. Sydney had no problem with this and often helped bridge the gap. And there were also times when her direct approach was too much. There were occasionally tears on the part of the coaches or the players. She had her share of fierce conversations with parents out of earshot of their daughters. She asked several to leave their program.

But what was difficult for some also made her worthy of respect with others, who knew her no-nonsense style was like a brick wall. The Beach's general manager made her the director of coaching, and with it came a raise. After barely three weeks on the job, she was making a serious impact on the operations of the gym.

The competition for college-level play was even worse than when she was in high school. College scholarship monies had to be shared across several women's sports teams now, not just volleyball. And while volleyball was popular, it didn't bring in the revenue for the schools like football, baseball or sometimes soccer. This increased pressure made it so a girl who might be talented would have no chance competing for the best schools unless she had more than just school team experience. Sydney's summer camp program filled up within days after it was announced on their website.

Sydney began a scholarship for players who could not afford the league fees, subsidized by several local businesses. It was just a small first start to something she hoped would expand. She began to talk about their programs at civic group meetings, and a very favorable article was printed in the local newspaper.

When it came time to promote their league season launch party, she created a volunteer group to do community outreach. Their group targeted some neighborhoods with high refugee populations where she knew funds would be lacking, and she'd met several promising young players who would never have been exposed to volleyball or have had a chance at a college scholarship.

It was delivering on the promise to the community as well as her personal convictions that sports for young women was very important to their develop-ment. She wanted to see that every girl who wanted to play could find a team regardless of the family's financial situation. It made her proud to be part of such an organization and to share her American lifestyle, especially with those who sought sanctuary in this country.

And although making the AVP circuit was still her goal, she could see a life for herself outside her own volleyball play.

The new work must be satisfying, she thought, because each night she crashed into bed, often forgetting to change into her night clothes. Mornings came too soon.

But then she began to feel her energy waning during the play. Carly noticed and, true to their commitment to each other, one day after practice spoke the truth that Sydney was just becoming aware of.

"You getting enough sleep, Sydney?" She poured water over her head and waited for her answer.

"God yes. That's all I do when I get home. I'm beginning to think working with so many people, you know, the coaches, parents, and the players, it's taken more out of me than I'd thought."

"You just seem to run out of steam. Not like before."

"I'm adjusting. We both have a lot on our plate."

But over the next week, she began wondering when the tiredness would go away, and if there wasn't something more serious wrong with her.

Alex was leaving for a two-week training exercise in Alaska, and hinted perhaps he'd come up for a quick visit the following weekend, which thrilled her. She lay in bed, dreaming what it would be like to see him again, and mourning the fact she wouldn't be able to talk to him for what seemed like an eternity. Watching the reflection of the early morning sun play across her ceiling, she shook her head at what a sap she'd become. How she'd worried he was perhaps losing interest. She almost felt lazy, wallowing in—what was it? Whatever she and Alex had to work out, she was confident their next meeting would send all the doubts away.

Showtime!

She rolled out of bed, stood to stretch, and immediately was hit with nausea. She ran to the bathroom and threw up, but as she looked at her face in the mirror afterward, she realized she could count on one hand the number of times she'd been that sick to her stomach.

And then she knew. Of course, she'd have to verify it, but the way she'd been feeling over the past days came flooding back to her.

On her way to the gym she stopped by the drug store. After her morning setup routine, she went into the stall bathroom and conducted the urine test and watched the results appear with her own eyes.

I'm pregnant.

CHAPTER 24

ALEX HAD BEEN ruminating over the discussion he'd had with Kyle and Lieutenant Garrison two weeks before.

"We think you might have what it takes, son, to be part of our DevGru Team. You'd have to try out, of course, and I won't lie, most men find it even more challenging than the BUD/S training. Question is, is this something you can see yourself doing?"

He watched Kyle's stoic face and was given neither encouragement nor doubt. Kyle was going to leave it entirely up to him.

"I'd be lying if I said I wasn't flattered." Alex had met a couple of the Team 6 guys at joint operations before their last deployment. They were the stuff of legends. They were often referred to as the professional players. Kyle's group was one of the best squads of any of the Teams, but DevGru was the place where the big boys played and played hard. He knew them also to be made up of a bunch of crazies who occasionally strayed off the farm.

"You think it over. It will be four months before the physical tryouts. We have about the same percentage of passes as BUD/S, so you'll want to get into the best shape of your life, or it will literally kick you on your butt. You understand?"

"Yes, sir."

"I have things I have to go over on my end if you decide to give it a try, so make sure you come with a firm decision."

"How long do I have?"

Kyle stood up from his perch sitting on the edge of the Lieutenant's desk. "Most men say yes to the LT, Kowicki. But the formal answer to that question is, *yesterday.*"

That little conversation had changed his entire focus. All of a sudden, he had to ask himself if he was ready for that level of commitment. He couldn't deny that he'd found a family in SEAL Team 3, and leaving them would be like cutting off his arm. If he didn't make the workup, there was also no guarantee there'd be a spot on Kyle's squad if he detached.

He was hesitant to discuss it with any of his bachelor friends. Coop was off at a medical training in North Carolina. Lucas was still having child custody issues with his ex, Connie. The ensuing battle was postponing his marriage to Marcy. That's all Lucas talked about, and it used to entertain him but now was annoying. Danny was settling in with Ali, getting his medical checkup and shots and dealing with a host of issues he'd inherited by bringing the boy stateside without permission. No one had the heart to tell him he couldn't come with Danny, but the fallout was considerable. It was even threatening Danny's career.

So Alex decided to risk a conversation with Kyle.

"I can't help you there, Kowicki. Just some guys know it's for them. For me, when they asked me, I'd just made this Team's LPO, which is what they do. They not only want leaders, but good operators too."

"How did you decide?"

"I didn't look at them and say to myself, *hey, that's me.*"

"You think it has to be a calling?"

"It's for guys who think of nothing else. I'm not that guy, Alex. I got Christy, the kids. But even before Christy was in the picture, I knew there would be someone, and I wasn't sure I could put them behind my career."

That gave even more for Alex to think about.

"Don't let him force you, muscle you. Make sure it's your decision. But you know, if you do it, give it everything you've got. You decide once. Everything else is execution."

"Thanks, Kyle. Appreciate it."

"One more thing. The new little lady. How tight are we there?"

Alex smirked. "She's pretty damned good for me, Kyle. But she's focused, like we are. She has some goals to achieve before anything else can happen in her life. I wouldn't want to be the one to get in the way of that."

"So, she'd be okay with it?"

"Does it matter? I mean, I've heard some of the wives don't take to it."

"No, they don't. So will that be okay if that happens, Alex? Gotta know the answer to that question."

"I guess I better find out."

"Roger that. But don't forget, it's your decision. It's not a democracy. You're the one who knows whether or not you want it. And that better not be situational, Alex. You gotta love it no matter what."

"Thanks."

"Oh, and by the way, congratufuckinlations! That's awesome they asked you."

OVER THE COURSE of the next couple of weeks, he'd wondered what Sydney would say if she knew he was considering this new assignment. Of course, he might wash out. Would she be okay with that?

But then he kicked himself around the block a bit. *Since when do you have to get permission from anyone when it comes to your career?* Perhaps it was not a very good sign he was considering her opinion at all. He was an elite warrior, doing what most other men could never do. The last line of defense. Wasn't that a higher calling?

And then the doubts would begin flooding in. His old self was scolding him, just like Joanne or his mother would, asking how he could be so callused.

Alex decided he needed to settle some things between himself and the other women in his life. He called and asked for a meeting at his mom's house.

JOANNE LOOKED PALE and had lost weight. "You okay, sis?"

"Of course I am."

She worked in a Catholic school that provided convent housing. He honored the fact that she had the will to be of service, putting her own needs behind the needs of others, but he knew she still harbored ill feelings for all the needling he'd done growing up. And he didn't think she was happy, really happy.

"Don't get into it with your sister, Alex," said his mom. "We all live in glass houses."

If there were two polar opposites, his mother and his sister would be at different ends of the scale. His mother was bright, attractive, highly opinionated, cynical and undisciplined. Her somewhat unconventional lifestyle had always bothered him. She didn't surround herself with big thinkers, but she had a saint for a daughter. Alex felt that was a burden to her, a thorn in her side.

"So what's so big you have to call a meeting?" his mom said as she lit up her cigarette.

"Mom!" squawked Joanne.

"Oh, come on, you know I've been a smoker for over twenty years."

"I think what Joanne is saying is although it's *your* habit, she has to inhale it too." Alex knew his mother would find fault with this. He wasn't wrong.

"Oh, Christ!" She put her cigarette out without apologizing for the swearing either. Joanne rolled her eyes.

"Well," started Alex, "now we can see why we don't get together much anymore." He stood and paced in front of the women. Joanne was examining her hands in her lap.

Alex knew the meeting was a waste of time. He was suddenly filled with regret for having called it. He didn't want to talk about his invitation to try out for SEAL Team 6.

"Just thought we should be more in touch," he lied.

"Which is code for you've met someone," his mother said.

"No, Mom. Well, yes, I have, but that wasn't the

reason I'm here."

"You don't fool me one bit, Alex. So you're going to dangle this little relationship in front of my nose? I've been asking you when you were going to get married for now—what—four years?"

"Probably longer," Joanne mumbled.

"Ever since I was out of diapers."

His mom chuckled at that comment.

Alex looked at the two of them seated on the purple velvet couch in his mother's small living room. Like everything surrounding her, the room was filled with splashes of color so bright it nearly hurt his eyes. No wonder she'd never remarried. No one would be able to stand living here, he thought.

He scratched the back of his neck. He hated being in these kinds of conversations. Sticky, undefined, everyone coming at him from different directions with motives he didn't trust. If this was family life, he never wanted anything to do with that. He'd rather get his teeth drilled without Novocain than have to spend a significant amount of time around these two women.

What the hell was I thinking?

Sydney was just as strong-willed, but she was—spectacular. That was the word he'd used to describe her to other Team guys. And even in her spectacularness, his mother would get a royal charge out of her zombie and chocolate fetish. That would be something he'd actually like to see.

His mother stood and came over to him. Putting her palm to his cheek, she began, "Alex, it's not that hard. Her name is…?" She waited, her eyebrows tented up.

He carefully peeled his mother's hand away. "Her name is Sydney. She's a beach volleyball player."

His mother smiled. "She wears those skimpy suits, all tanned and buttered up all the time." Her eyes sparkled with glee.

"Mother!" Alex shouted.

Joanne scowled at him, then faced his mother. "What is the matter with you? Let him say it in his own way. You're making him feel like an insect in a jar."

Alex was grateful his sister thought to stick up for him. "Like a camel spider," he added.

Both women looked up to him and said in unison, "What?"

"I saw one over in Iraq. Ugly things. Look like potato bugs, you know with the funny legs and big blue-green bodies." The women weren't reacting, so he added, "My co-worker sat on one."

"You see, Joanne, if you let him talk, this is what he does." His mother spoke to his sister like he wasn't in the room. He hated that.

Joanne looked up to him like she'd used to when they were kids. He saw a warmth there he hadn't seen for many years. "I'm ready to listen, Alex, when you're ready to talk about it. I'm not judging you. Just want you to know that."

"Thank you." He meant it. "Her name is Sydney, as I've said. I like her a lot." He opened his palms. "And there you have it. That's what I came to say."

All the way home he felt like a shit. Confusion wasn't natural for him. Only thing he knew to settle his nerves was to go for a skydive. Maybe his mother was right after all. All of them were freaks.

It just seemed like he should tell someone he was seriously considering doing something so dangerous that most men turned it down. He wasn't most men. His family wasn't like most families, either.

No, he knew who he needed to discuss this decision with. He'd been putting off the meeting, and now it was time. When he came back from Alaska he'd see her, and let her know how much he appreciated their time together.

And then he'd end the relationship. He had no business asking anyone to wait for him or grieve when he was gone. Besides, he was just learning how to get over his childhood. And this would give Sydney time to pursue her dreams without the distraction of worrying about where he was and what he was doing.

Now you're justifying again, you asshole. Maybe it was easier to commit to the SEALs than to a woman, even a spectacular woman like Sydney.

He hoped the cold of Alaska would freeze that burden out of him permanently.

Yup. Jumping out of an airplane at thirteen thousand feet today was sounding pretty good right now.

CHAPTER 25

S YDNEY DIDN'T TELL Carly about her pregnancy or the clinic appointment. She wanted unequivocal proof before she'd start talking about it with anyone. Faced with the choices she had to make, the decision whether or not to have the baby weighed heavily on her. She knew Alex would have a reaction and had a right to know. She knew it was the right thing to tell him, but she wasn't sure what effect it would have on their relationship. How much should that weigh on her decision?

And then, of course, was the issue of her AVP goals. That would also impact Carly. The Beach had stuck their neck out for her, giving her a safe space to train, to afford to live, to have whatever it was she wanted of her future goals. She told herself that included Alex, but this was totally not what she'd expected, having been on the pill.

Now she understood the difficulties other single

women had in making this decision. It was ultimately a decision she had to live with the rest of her life. While she was thrilled at the possibility of raising a child of Alex's, it wasn't right to do that without his input. And she'd always disliked the decision others made to terminate a pregnancy. She thought the decision would be an easy one for her, but now she knew the truth of it.

The clinic was filled to bursting with pregnant women, usually alone, but occasionally with a mother or a boyfriend or husband. Some of the women were very young, not much older than the girls she worked with on her teams at the Beach.

She tried not to study the faces of the girls waiting, as if the burden or the joy of their situation would somehow affect her.

Her name was called by a hoarse woman in a lab coat covering blue jeans and a T-shirt. Suddenly, she felt guilty for not having waited to get a proper doctor's appointment in a discreet, private office somewhere.

But she wasn't one to shirk her responsibilities. Pregnancy had been the least of her worries when they were having unprotected sex. She'd been stupid. Really stupid, she thought as she followed the woman to the exam room.

"How far along are you?"

"Not long. Less than a month."

She was directed toward a chair. "So you've missed one period?"

"Oh my God. I didn't even think of that. I play sports, and sometimes when I'm heavily training, like now, I don't have one for several months.

"You must be aware of the fact that nearly a third of all pregnancies terminate themselves in the first trimester, right?"

"Yes, I think I knew that. I did the home test, and it came out positive. I repeated it again yesterday and the results were the same."

She answered a number of questions as the clerk went down the list of items on the form Sydney had filled out while waiting. She held her emotions inside and told herself she was here for the facts, that the decision didn't have to be made today or even this week. She'd be out of contact with Alex for another week. She was hoping that time would point her in the right direction.

"Any discharge, cramping?"

"No."

"We'll have to do a physical exam, but probably not today. You're sure on the dates?"

"Positive."

"Okay, let's get the blood test done. I'll need a urine sample too."

She was given a plastic cup and shown the way to

the bathroom. The clerk had her wait while she dipped the test strip into her urine. It came out bright blue.

"That would be a yes," the woman said.

They made plans for a follow-up visit. Sydney was given a packet of information on the services they provided at the clinic. "So you can make an informed decision. I'm required to give you all of this, even if you're going to go through with having the baby. And we have counselors' phone numbers on the backside here and other resources too, all listed."

She thanked the clerk, took her packet and her appointment card and walked out through the waiting room without looking at a soul. The outcome was what she'd expected. She was waiting for her emotions to show up. But she'd done such a good job stuffing them down, they were MIA.

It wasn't until she saw a young mother with a baby in a Snugli pack that she felt her eyes ache and then tear up. Inhaling deeply and looking away helped. She'd way underestimated the flood of images of her father, family photographs she'd seen growing up and then cherished when he was gone. She knew what he'd say, what he'd be thinking if he were here. And she felt ashamed she was even considering the cruel alternative—something she was sure she'd regret the rest of her life.

At home that night, she put the brochure into the

top drawer next to her bed and tucked it away, deciding for now she was going to put it all out of her mind. The first person she would tell was going to be here in a week. Then she'd go from there.

ALEX WAS COMING in on the eight-thirty direct flight from San Diego. She needed to pee again as she shifted her balance between feet, her hands tucked into her fleece jacket pockets. She didn't want to appear nervous, but she couldn't stop from sweating, and her breathing hitched unevenly as if she couldn't get enough air. Her mouth was parched. Her stomach lurched when she watched his plane land. She dug her hands out, placing them on the glass divider, leaving foggy handprints from her heat as she examined the string of passengers exiting the plane.

There was no mistaking Alex from everyone else around him. Not the tallest of men, he was certainly the best built, and with his sharp dark features and strong jawline, he was the one people noticed. Men moved away from him, giving him a wide berth, as if knowing what he did for a living. Women did double takes, sometimes whispering to the person beside them. It would forever be hard for Alex to walk into a room and not make the whole place sigh. She imagined him dressed to the nines, wearing a tux.

His long gait made fast work of the distance between them. His smile warmed her whole body. She held back the tears and regretted she couldn't just run and tell him about the pregnancy. Sydney was going to have to pretend everything was status quo until the right time. Playing this little game of hide and seek, which might have been thrilling in their past encounters as the sparks engulfed them, now felt dishonest. She had always been so sure of herself. Now she had to do the right thing, whatever that was, and worry she'd send him away, never to return.

In the warm embrace and the chaste kiss at the side of her face when he entered the lobby of the airport, she lost herself in the scent of the man she ached to love. She hated the barriers that now loomed large between them.

"Welcome back," she whispered, her arm wrapped around his waist, her head leaning into his shoulder.

His answer shocked her. "Thanks."

Not, *It's good to be back,* or *Missed you.*

"Where are you parked?" His voice was warm, but efficient. Something was wrong. A wave of nausea began at the pit of her stomach as her spine became stiff, her skin clammy, and her emotions prickly. Underneath it all was not only dread, but anger.

She handed him the keys, and he opened the door for her, placing his large bag in the second seat. Walking around to the driver's door, she saw through the windshield he was staring off into the distance and his left eye was narrowed, his lips pursed.

Instinctively she lay her hands against her stomach, willing it to stop flip-flopping between excitement and nausea. As soon as he'd strapped in and turned on the engine, she removed her hands and breathed in a wish upon that star that had always done so well for her. She didn't know what she was praying or wishing for. It was just a thought.

Please.

Alex cleared his throat. "Sydney, I have some things to bring to Nick. We didn't talk about arrangements, so they have the bunkhouse set up for me."

She whipped her head around, storm clouds brewing just above her eyebrows. "You're staying *there?* But I thought—"

He pulled over to the curb. They had neared the toll gate exit from the parking lot. He got out his wallet.

"It's free." She handed him the ticket. "Just give him this."

Their eyes made contact as he pulled the ticket from her fingers. Too late she'd discovered she was holding onto the paper, and he had to do a last minute tug.

His eyes softened before he answered her. "I know how busy you are. I just thought it would be easier."

She broke away and peered out the windshield at a

pretty blue sky and green vineyard day, at a world that was moving along so normally. And she wasn't a part of it. The disappointment and anger building made it easy to control the tears that had been threatening. She didn't look at him when she answered, "We've not seen each other for over a month. You've been overseas on a dangerous mission you can't talk about. I've been working hard to focus on the training and all that supports it. These were the goals we stated when you left. These were the things we said we wanted to accomplish when we spoke on the phone."

He was heading to the toll booth, rolling down the window, when she turned to him and asked, "What's changed?"

He continued through the frontage road, towards the direction of the freeway. "I didn't want you to feel like you had to entertain me."

"And why not? You didn't seem to mind last time you were here." She held back the venom she was feeling.

His chuckle began to melt her frostiness. "No, that's true, Sydney. Those were some mighty wonderful times, and I think of them often." She saw his smile in profile.

"So where's the but?"

"I didn't want you to feel obligated, you know, just in case—"

"Just in case I'd changed my mind about seeing you? You honestly think that would be anywhere within the realm of possibility? Alex, just level with me. Have you changed your mind? What am I missing here?"

Sydney watched as he peeled off the freeway to the country road his friend's winery must be on.

"We need to talk. I'm crazy about you, Sydney." He grabbed her hand. "Your hands are cold." He kissed her knuckles, which further melted her defensive exterior. "But some things have happened, and we need to talk first. This time, we *have* to talk."

No kidding!

"So, I'm going to drop off the things I brought for Nick, and then maybe you and I can go have a private chat somewhere."

His cell phone chirped. Sydney could hear a man's voice on the other end. It sounded like Nick was telling him they were on their way to the hospital.

"That's great news, man. We're probably ten minutes away. I'll drop off your order if someone can let me in."

There was chatter.

"That'll work. Give me the name of the hospital." He turned to Sydney. "Santa Rosa Memorial? Okay, I think we can find it. Maybe see you in an hour? Give you a chance to settle in?"

She heard more chatter. "Well, call me if something changes. Hey, man, congratulations! You're almost a father. That's cool. Very cool."

Sydney looked out the passenger window as they wound under the freeway and down the two-lane country road.

"Well, that kind of changes things a bit. They're off to have their baby. Mind if we stop by?"

"Of course not," she said to the window.

She felt his hand on her shoulder, shaking her slightly. "You okay? Everything okay?"

"Everything's fine."

When she didn't look him in the face, he dropped his hand. Soon, they were at the gravel driveway of Sophie's Choice Winery. She remarked how beautiful the golden hills were that bordered the bucolic valley of green vineyards and olive trees. They came upon a field of lavender before arriving at the tasting room entrance. A large water fountain embellished the entrance. The parking lot was empty. Alex drove around the side to the back where several modern structures and a warehouse were located.

From his large bag, Alex took out a long black nylon zipper case Sydney recognized was for a long gun. "I'll give you a tour," he said.

The back door to the main house was open. He took her hand. "You'll love this place. Come on."

He seemed to warm the longer they were inside. Alex led her up the wooden staircase to a set of double doors leading to the master bedroom. He placed the case on the floor of a walk-in closet. A large four-poster bed dwarfed the room. Antiques and hand-hewn furniture decorated the space. The ambiance of the home was lovely.

"There's Devon's office down there. Nick has one of the spare bedrooms up here for his. Downstairs they have a guest room and bath." He grabbed her hand tighter this time. Her unease was beginning to dissipate. They stopped at the top of the staircase, overlooking the living/dining/kitchen great room downstairs. Straight across were clearstory windows showing the lush green of the rows of vines. "You like?"

The whole house and surrounding property made her breathless. "What's not to like? It's incredible. So this, this is what you guys were talking about doing up here?"

He gave a half laugh. "You understand Nick and Devon have been working on it for several years. All her income and what he inherited from his sister went into making this place what it is today. Took a lot of work and a lot of money. We don't have the luxury of either. But we're working on it."

"But this is the inspiration, the vision, right?" She

felt the heat from his body as she stood close to him. She leaned against the railing bending one knee so that when their eyes met, they were level to each other. He watched her mouth as if it was the first time he'd noticed her.

The tug of the chemistry between them was still there. His hand came up to the back of her head as he pressed his lips to hers. She let her inner demon out and pulled him into her, which made him chuckle through the deepening kiss. "Don't tell me you're staying anywhere else but my bed, sailor. Don't you dare tell me that."

"Well, all right," was his answer. His sigh was music to her ears. He was falling into the urgency of their proximity to each other. The attraction was undeniable and just as strong as it had ever been.

And then he pulled away. "Come on. We have to talk." He led her down the stairs to the kitchen, pulled out two glasses and poured them each ice water from the dispenser, handing one to her. "Just a minute while I check on something first." He disappeared around the corner and returned a minute later. "Zak and Amy are up here. Thought maybe they were staying in the guest room. But we're alone."

Sydney sat and waited for whatever he was going to tell her. The knowledge that he'd not lost his feelings for her buoyed her spirits. But something had come between them, and there were some things she feared more than others.

Alex pulled up a chair made out of rustic branches from a pine tree, and sat across from her, his knees touching hers. She leaned forward. Whatever he was going to tell her, she was going to face head-on. She was anxious to get it over with.

"I've been invited to try out for the DevGru Team. That's more commonly known as SEAL Team 6, although the group has special forces from other branches as well. Kind of a boys' club with all the badasses in all branches. They do all the high-level stuff, not that we don't on Kyle's team, but these guys, these guys are the best of the best."

"Okay. So what does that mean?"

"Well, I have to try out. They have to vet me as well, with interviews. Someone high up must have recommended me, because you don't ask to be on one of these, and it's an honor to even be approached."

"I'm proud of you, Alex. That's quite an honor."

"It is." He leaned in further, taking her hands in his. "But it means I will be gone much more. It also means I could be gone for longer periods, part of that in training missions or training other forces. I wouldn't really have a home life, so to speak."

She was beginning to understand what he'd been struggling with. It pained her, but she realized he was telling her she would not, could not, be as prominent in his life as perhaps she wanted, or they'd planned on. This was the change pushing him away.

"And you think I'll be whining at home, baggage under your feet. You do know I have my own set of plans."

"Yes, that's why I thought perhaps this would work. But as much as I'd love to just move forward with us, if I take this job, our relationship, everything about us has to go on hold."

"So this is for uncommitted guys."

"No. Some are married, but they came into the program married. Or they sorted it out and got married. But what I'm saying is that I can't do both right now. And I don't want you to sit with any false promises or expectations. I might not make it, which means maybe I'd be reassigned to another team, maybe back East. If I do, I wouldn't be home much for the first couple of years. This is more than a full-time job. And it requires my complete attention. Complete."

Their eyes met again. She found it in herself to not show him the disappointment she felt. What she showed him instead was how proud she was, because that was there too.

"So you've told them yes, then?"

"In a manner of speaking. I've not filled out the paperwork. I've talked it over with Kyle, and, Sydney, I'd like to try doing this. I'll never know if I don't give it a shot."

Now she knew she wouldn't be able to tell him about her secret. He'd made up his mind without her counsel, which was totally appropriate. So that meant she had to make the same decision for herself without counseling him. But it still didn't sit right with her. She knew then and there she was going to have this baby, with or without Alex at her side. And she'd have to wait to tell him.

That was the hardest thing of all. Telling Carly would be a piece of cake compared to that. But some day, when the time was right, she'd tell him. But that day wasn't today.

"Go for it, Alex. I hear what you're saying and not saying. You're asking me not to wait for you, that you might not want me when you're done. I understand the stakes, believe me. And maybe this is as close as we're ever going to be."

He released her hands and sat up straighter.

"I—I guess you're right. I didn't think about that."

It was so incredibly hard, but she'd find the strength within herself to make him fall in love with her all over again. Make it hurt when he went away. Make him find he needed her more than ever, and he'd for sure come back. If there ever was going to be a chance for them, her job would be to blow his mind so that he'd never forget her. "So what you're saying is your ass is mine this weekend and then I got to get over you."

He started to object, but she cut him off.

"Ah?" She put her finger in the air. "Hear me out. If you come back, and I've met someone else, you'll have to accept it, right?"

"Well—"

"It *has* to be that way, Alex. You have to give me the same freedom you are asking me for."

"Well, I guess that sounds fair. Sydney, I'm not sending you away."

"Oh, but you are. You're telling me that your job is going to come first. I get it now." She sucked in a big gulp of air, masking her nervousness. "I can do this on one condition."

"And that is?"

"If we're agreeing to walk away after this weekend, you better show up, at least for the next two days. I mean fully. Do we have a deal?"

CHAPTER 26

ALEX HELD HER hand as they drove to the hospital. "This will be a first for me," he said, kissing her knuckles.

"Me too."

Sydney had been quiet. He couldn't believe how incredibly understanding she'd been. He was expecting the weekend to be painful, and then he'd go home to San Diego, sign all the paperwork to start the application for SEAL Team 6, and just move on with his life, trying to forget her. That was for her sake, not his. Otherwise, he'd have a weak moment between tours or trainings, look her up, have a weekend of sex and then not be able to offer her anything else—going back to work and knowing he used her. He respected her too much to do that to her.

So he'd also decided not to try to force himself on her, arranging to stay at Nick and Devon's. That felt like taking too much advantage of her.

So why am I here then?

Because he wasn't a heel. He wasn't going to just give her the phone call, or write a letter and end it. She deserved to hear it from him in person. When he'd left for Iraq so much had been unspoken, but he knew she felt it too.

When the DevGru guys contacted him, suddenly he found he was willing to put himself through that one more test. He wanted her to understand that. And he thought now she did.

He hadn't considered *this* alternative she gave him. The good-bye weekend. Something special to remember each other by. It was beyond his wildest dreams that he'd finally met someone who was okay letting him be who he wanted to be and not some stuffed-shirt replica of her idea of the perfect boyfriend. He could walk away with no regrets, and the best part of it was she could too.

She was the strongest woman he'd ever met.

He didn't want to think too far out into the future, but he could see that after the next couple of years, they could seriously have one together. As long as he wasn't pressured before that time.

He also liked that she had something she was as passionate about as he did. She wasn't living her life through him, depending on him to bring it to her. She had her own. How had he gotten so lucky?

As the minutes passed, he found it safer to touch her, to hold her hand. He felt her unthaw as well. Her stiffness had gone away, her smiles had returned, and she became more lighthearted. Suddenly the weekend looked to be a real adventure. He might even suggest another zombie movie. She'd love that! And he'd let her bring it on however she liked, as long as it was started on her side of the fence.

The Labor and Delivery unit was on the third floor. A check-in volunteer led them to a cozy waiting room which was empty. The attendant left after promising she'd let Nick and Devon know they were waiting.

"Hey there, Alex!" Nick was dressed in blue jeans. Alex expected he'd be in scrubs or something sterile, so he hesitated to give him a hug. The two were not close friends yet, but the occasion was a celebratory one, so they embraced quickly. "So how's it going? Is it baby time yet?" asked Alex.

"No. We have a ways to go. But right now, Alex, I'm higher than a kite, right there with her, man."

"Where's Zak? Thought he was staying with you guys."

"Haven't been able to get hold of him yet. But they're staying with Amy's dad. A couple other guys from Team 3 came up yesterday. They're probably partying." Nick stuck out his hand, reaching for Sydney. "We've not been introduced, but man, I feel like I know you from somewhere."

"Oh God, I'm sorry," Alex blurted out. "Nick, this is Sydney Robinson. Sydney, Nick Dunn."

Sydney shook Nick's hand and smiled. "You've probably seen me play on the beach down south."

"I've been up here almost three years now. I'm thinking it was that sports magazine cover? The one where you were—" He demonstrated by raising his arm from the shoulder, elbow high in the air, with his back arched. "That was you, wasn't it? Little yellow thong, showed waay too much?" He quickly checked with Alex and then finished in a whisper. "I had that picture on my locker at Gunny's before I moved up here and got married."

Alex knew just what picture that was since Sydney had it framed on her bedroom wall in San Diego. He'd stared at it that morning after.

Sydney blushed and put her hands on her hips, slouched to one side since she towered over both of them. Alex could see she liked Nick. "I'd love to be in that kind of shape again someday." She glanced at Alex. "I'm going to go use the restroom, if you don't mind, okay?"

"Sure."

Nick tilted on his heels to get a good shot of Sydney walking down the hallway. He shook his head and punched Alex in the arm. "Don't know how you guys do it."

Alex ignored him and asked about Devon.

"She's a trooper. She's already dilated four centimeters."

Alex had no clue what that meant.

"When Sydney comes back, I'll let you guys go in and see her."

"Whoa, no way, man. This is your time. I'm not going to infringe on that. Besides, I've just come from a plane stuffed with people. We're only here to give you moral support."

"Oh relax, Alex. Not like she's naked and you're going to see her parts and all. She's in a nightgown, except she has monitors stuck to her all over under her gown."

Sydney returned.

"Nick says we can go in and visit for a little bit. You want to?"

"I don't want to impose. Sort of a strange time to meet someone when she's in labor and all. I'm not sure I'd want to meet strangers under those conditions."

"Oh, she's totally fine. She said you guys could come in. The nurses are cool with it too. Whatever keeps her calm." Nick motioned for them to follow. A nurse stopped him in the hallway, and he told her his wife was expecting them.

Devon's hair was done up in pigtails, like the day

he'd attended the wedding at the winery. "Hi there, Alex. I guess today's the day!"

Her face was flushed, and her forehead had wetted her bangs. She had a bright red floral shawl over her shoulders. The light in the room was turned down low and some sea music was playing on her cell phone.

Alex leaned over the bed and gave her a peck on the cheek. "Hey, Mama. You look beautiful."

"Oh please, you're such a liar."

Once again, he'd forgotten to introduce Sydney. Devon was angling to be able to greet her. "You must be Sydney."

Alex put his arm around Sydney's shoulders and then brought her toward the bed.

"Nice meeting you. I—I hadn't planned on barging in here. So sorry."

"Oh, nonsense," said Devon as she made a face and exhaled. "Hold that thought for a minute. Here comes another one." She leaned back into the pillow. Nick was at her shoulders, giving her an upper spine massage, running his fingers up the back of her neck and into her hair. She took deep breaths, letting it out slowly until the contraction appeared to be over.

"How long's it going to be?" Sydney asked.

"We have no idea. But she's coming along. We're making progress, aren't we, sweetie?" Nick squeezed his wife's hand.

"It's up to the baby. We're on her time," Devon said.

Sydney spoke up again. "You know it's a girl?"

"Nope. I want a girl. He wants a boy. We don't care. It's a friendly argument."

Nick was perched on the edge of Devon's bed. "Have a seat for a little bit. You want something? They have custard and Jell-o down at the nurses' station. Other stuff too I don't want to tempt her with."

"No, we're fine," answered Alex. "But can I get you something, Devon?"

"I'd love a cool towel for my forehead."

Before the men could get up, Sydney was at the sink wetting down one of the folded washcloths stacked neatly there. She squeezed it tightly, then brought it over to Devon's face. "Here you go." She pressed the white cloth to her forehead, lifting her bangs before doing so. She dabbed her cheeks, then under her chin, across her lips and down her neck to the top of her chest. "That feel better?" she asked.

"Heavenly."

Alex watched Sydney's tenderness. Something about the scene touched him. Some kind of invisible bond had already formed between the two women. It added to his respect for the mystique of womanhood. He wondered why some women had it and others, like his mother, didn't seem to have a clue. Or maybe she'd stopped trying when life got too hard at home.

"Devon, Sydney is a beach volleyball player," Nick whispered. He turned up the noise of the ocean. "This probably makes you feel at home too, Sydney," he added.

"It actually does," said Sydney.

A nurse came in. "I'm gonna ask all of you to go outside now while I give her a check. You can come back when I finish updating her chart."

Alex, Nick, and Sydney exited to the waiting room. A very young father was on a cell phone even though signs posted around the room advised all phones be turned off.

The trio walked through the double swinging doors back into the lobby just outside the surgery waiting room which was three times bigger.

"So how long are you up here for?" Nick finally asked.

"Just today, tomorrow and part of Sunday, when I go back."

"Oh, that's too bad. I'm sure Devon would have wanted you to see all the things she's discovered about the property. Zak and Amy have already started with cleanup. Supposed to get the appraisal done next week."

"I guess Coop's in-laws are investing in it too?"

"Think so. We'll need a final head count and tally

of moneys we have to work with, but Devon says they want us to have the property. Zak's got several of the single guys agreeing to come up here occasionally for a work party."

Alex wanted to know about Zak. He was hoping the transition to civilian life wouldn't be hard on him, especially with the loss of his eye.

Nick reassured him. "Seems to feel quite at home. We've been talking about labels, which is getting way ahead of ourselves. Something with the pirate theme, maybe a drawing of Zak with his eye patch."

"Pirate piss wine."

"Actually, we were thinking about brewing some beer too. We kind of liked the name Frog Piss, maybe make it green or put it in green bottles."

"I'm glad he's adjusting." Nick went into detail about the land while Alex watched Sydney. She observed several pregnant couples arriving at the birthing center. Another woman dressed in a hospital gown like Devon's was walking between a man and an older woman who appeared to be her mother.

Sydney caught him watching her, and abruptly she looked away.

Nick discovered he was being ignored and started asking Alex questions about their visit to Iraq.

"You got Ali, right?"

"We sure did. None too soon, either. We took out

four bad guys, one kid really young, the rest teenagers. Nobody high level, or at least the DNA didn't give us anyone we knew about. We think they were there just to make sure the kids or the aid workers didn't escape. Our terp said they expected someone big to arrive and choose which children to take."

"Sick bastards. Glad you got out without injury."

"Me too. And it helps when we get accurate intel. That doesn't always happen anymore."

Nick agreed, but refocused his attention on Sydney. "So how do you like it up here? It's different than San Diego."

"It suits me fine. Got a great training partner, and the facility is awesome. Ever heard of it? Beach Inc."

Nick shook his head.

"They have four sand courts in addition to the regular gym floor. That's where I train. But I'm also the director of coaching, so I get to work with girls of all ages, from just starting out to gals from Sonoma State and the J.C."

"I'll bet you were a find for them, then."

Sydney rolled her shoulder and shrugged. "It's the perfect arrangement."

"Well, after the baby's born, we'll have to come down and watch you play."

"Thanks. Even Alex hasn't seen that yet." She winked at him.

The nurse poked her head outside the double doors and told them she was finished with Devon. Sydney held Alex back.

"I don't want to stay too long. I don't care if she wants us there, I'd like to give them private time."

"No complaints from me." He slipped his arm around her waist. "You doing okay?"

She darted a quick look at him, low-level defensiveness showing just under the surface of her flawless tanned skin. "Sure. Why wouldn't I be?"

He squeezed her tighter to his side. "Just checking."

Devon was having another contraction as they walked back inside, and this one had her nearly swearing. Alex waited until she regained concentration to indicate he and Sydney would be leaving soon.

Sydney bent over and gave Devon a hug. "Best of luck. I understand being a mother is the hardest job you'll ever love. I know you two will make great parents, from all I've heard about you both. I'll be thinking of you today."

"Aww. Thank you, Sydney. What a lovely thing to say." Devon's face was flushed with a bright smile. "So glad I got to meet you on this special day." And then her face scrunched up as another contraction began.

Alex loved Sydney's soft features as she wafted past him, leaving the hospital room to wait for him outside in the hall. He felt awkward for a second, with Nick attending to his wife and Devon focused on her delivery. He gave a thumbs up, which Nick returned.

All the way down the corridor, down the elevator and across the parking lot, he held Sydney's hand loosely. Neither one said a word.

CHAPTER 27

YDNEY WAS MOVED by the hospital scene with Alex's friends. She'd been there to witness a miracle, the start of a new life, and she pondered the impact it would have on everyone around them. Even her.

She was even more sure of her decision than she had been earlier in the day. Something inside her soul had settled. And yet, there was so much unknown about the future. She was proud of herself. Instead of fear, she was changing, rising to the opportunity to face this new challenge with grace and dignity, bearing the emotions and the fear and doubt she knew would come along as hitchhikers for a time here and there. She wasn't being a Pollyanna about it. She stared reality in the face and reality blinked. She did not. Would not.

Out of the corner of her eye she could see Alex give her furtive glances. That was good, she told herself. He had noticed a change in her. It would be the first of many. She chuckled at the remembrance of their first date, only a few weeks ago. The zombie movie and the popcorn and—

"What in the devil are you thinking, Sydney?" he asked.

She examined his face in profile as he drove. "You'll take this off-ramp and go under the freeway here." She pointed and then went back to feasting on his handsome face. "I was thinking about our first date. And don't ask me why I thought about it just now."

"Why did you think about it just now?" he said with a grin.

"Funny."

"No, seriously. Why?"

"I can't believe I was so out of control."

Alex raised his eyebrows. "That's an understatement. I wasn't sure you were safe to be around."

She speculated on what he would look like in twenty years. He'd stay handsome, stay rugged-looking, and lose what little boyishness he had, which wasn't much. He'd probably stop getting tats, but maybe not. His hair would be streaked with white perhaps. She smoothed her fingers through his temple, letting them delve into his scalp, and then squeezed the back of his neck. "I think you'll be even more handsome when you're in your forties or beyond."

"And I think you'll always be that volleyball goddess everyone had pinned to their lockers."

"You think so?" She liked that at least he tried to lie for her benefit. It was a lie she could live with.

She finished the directions, and at last they came to the complex. He was at her side of the car in a flash and opened the door for her. As he leaned past her and grabbed his bag, the scent from the proximity to his muscled neck nearly made her weak at the knees. She resisted the urge to kiss him there, figuring there would be time for the fog of lust, if that was what was to occur. She was orchestrating something, now. There were things she urgently wanted, but she had to put some of them on hold. It actually felt good to be more in control of her emotions. She wanted to walk through the doorway of this day and remember it all. Remember tomorrow and Sunday. Remember how she felt on Monday and thereafter.

He walked beside her as they climbed the three flights. He was barely out of breath when they got to the outside of her apartment. She turned, her back flat against the door, her hips at an angle. "Kiss me, Alex."

He bent forward, dropping his bag and placing both hands at the side of her face and then nourished her with a loving kiss that sent chills all the way to her toes. She knew she'd always remember that special kiss. It was life-giving. She hoped the tiny child she was carrying could feel it too.

She placed her fingers over his mouth. "I love your kisses, Alex. I just want to say that."

"I have lots more."

"I was hoping so." Looking down, she examined her keys. "I want to take it a bit slow at first, if you don't mind. Not because I don't like the fun and the intensity of the other way, but I just want to honor our last weekend together."

Emotions were beginning to steep inside her, her heart fluttered a bit, as some of the old fear reared its head. Her eyes were beginning to water, but she faced him anyway and let him see all of her.

"Syd, I'll take it fast, slow, any way you want it. You have nothing to fear from me, sweetheart."

It would be so easy to just drown out all logic, let herself go, and set up the make-believe world of the Happily Ever After and deny herself the opportunity to show him what a real lady she was. Yes, she was a character. But she was also a lady, and she was going to be a mother, a task she willingly took on with pride. It didn't matter if her baby's birth day wasn't shared with him. He could be halfway around the world in some hellhole, doing things she didn't even want to know about. It would make it no less sacred a time. No less important. She'd make it the best day of her life, like today was for Devon and Nick.

Once inside, Alex watched her set her keys aside

and kick off her shoes, which was always her routine. He was still holding onto the canvas bag, the strap hanging from his shoulder.

"Where do I put this?" His sparkling eyes and little boy smile cheering her.

"Unless you'd rather sleep on the couch, I suggest the bedroom."

"Yes, ma'am." He'd left his jacket behind when he returned. He approached, wrapping his arms around her waist. His fingers removed a couple of long errant hairs from her forehead. "I'm getting used to kissing you on my tiptoes. The first time it happened, I wasn't so sure it would work for me."

She met him half way and they melded together as though there were no distance between them. Sydney took his hand and directed him to sit on the couch. She sat crossing him, her legs nearly touching the end. "I have a couple of ideas of some things we talked about. Some things I'd like to do this weekend, if you're game."

His large hand massaged the top of her spine, something she loved almost more than morning sex. "Okay, shoot."

"Wine tasting. There's the rugged coastline. Oysters at Marshall's Cove. You game for any of that?" she asked.

She noticed he was keeping his hands to himself.

"And I'd like to talk more. I want to know about you and your family."

"You mean you want my pedigree?"

She was embarrassed she'd come that close to coming right out and telling him she wanted to know what she would tell their child some day if he wasn't going to be in the picture. Sitting as she was on his lap, that seemed less likely. "You're being cute. There must be something you want to ask of me."

"Yes." He inhaled big and leaned forward, holding her face in his hands again and kissing her deep. "Among other things, I'd like to see you play volleyball."

"Really?"

"Yes ma'am. I'm as serious as a heart attack."

She scrambled to her feet, pulling him up. "Carly will be there now. If we go right now, we can show you what we're working on."

"I just want to watch you jump and spike and do all those things I've been fantasizing about in my mind. I couldn't stop thinking about it when I was over there."

"Let's do it. Let me get changed and we'll go, okay?"

"You need any help? It's been driving me crazy." He pulled her to him again. "I wasn't going to go anywhere near that, but honey, I'm afraid I'm a flawed man. I can't help myself."

She liked that he wanted to dally. Pressing her lips

to his, taking nibbles as she did so, she whispered, "We have all night, Alex. I promise to make it up to you, okay?"

He held her at arm's length and examined her face. "Going to make me wait?"

"The anticipation will make it sweeter. Trust me on this. If you want to see me play, we have to leave right now or we'll miss Carly."

"Call her."

"Good idea." She waved to him, standing there with his long arms down at his sides, his shirt halfway pulled out of his jeans, and his hair messed up. His lips had a bit of her red lipstick that lingered and made him look sexy as hell. Those eyes and his playful smile promised kisses she loved all over her body.

Carly didn't answer her cell, so she left a message. "Hey there, Alex and I are coming over, so don't go anywhere. He wants to get a personal tour and watch us play a bit. See if you can get some of the older girls to stay behind too. See you in like ten. Bye."

The sight of his black bag and jacket placed on her bedspread sparked her with excitement. She used the restroom quickly, then rummaged through the top dresser drawer where her underwear was located. She hadn't worn the little yellow outfit in over a year. She slid off her clothes, tossing them into her hamper in the closet, and then stepped into the tiny thong bottoms, sliding them up her flat abdomen, the arch of the panty coming just below her hip bone. Then she slipped the bra top over her head, pulling it down until it lifted and supported her breasts. She examined herself in the mirror, turning around to make sure everything looked right.

"Vera vera nice," Alex said wolfishly. "You're sure we couldn't fool around with this little outfit for a few minutes before you get it all hot and sweaty?"

"Oh, but I like things hot and sweaty," she said as she slipped past him, making sure to brush against his growing package. "All good things come to those who wait. And in this case, you won't have to wait very long. We'll do a late lunch, or just skip lunch and come back here. Unless you have a better idea."

Her fingers brushed over his lips again. He grabbed her arm and pressed her palm to the outside of his jeans.

"Nice," she whispered. "but if you want to see this gal jump and show off for you, your private volleyball player, you're gonna have to hold that thought until just a little later." She kissed him quickly. "Come on."

She stepped into her black workout pants and fleece jacket with the Beach Inc. logo on it, while he slipped on his jacket, taking something from his pocket, and then adjusting his waistband.

She slipped on her shoes, and they headed down

the stairway to her car.

The early afternoon traffic was heavy for a Friday. They got to the Beach in a little over twenty minutes. The parking lot was full of SUVs and only a couple of sedans. She recognized Mrs. Beeson's car. Two large white vans were backed into the rollup doors at the rear side of the building. Sydney didn't recall any tournaments scheduled or team scrimmages. Without markings and windows, she assumed perhaps a private delivery service was setting up some new equipment the general manager had ordered.

As they exited the Murano, Alex got a call from Zak. He placed his finger up in the air while he answered the phone.

"I'll go get warmed up. Take as long as you like," she whispered to him, then gave him a kiss on the cheek. She plugged her earbuds into her cell phone, unzipped her jacket and snapped the device into the Velcro holder on her arm. She liked warming up to the *Rocky* theme song and played it as she jogged toward the entrance.

Closer to the lobby, a mother with her child was walking back toward her. Sydney removed one ear bud.

"Oh, Sydney, thank goodness you're here. They've got it locked. I knocked and no one came," the mother said.

Sydney cocked her head, concerned. "Well, I have

the keys, let me open it for you. Someone's little sister must be fiddling with the door lock mechanism."

"Well, I know someone's inside, with all these cars out here," the mom said.

Sydney got out her keys and no sooner had she inserted the metal fob into the dead bolt when the door swung open and she was yanked into the dark cave of the dark gym. Someone else had the young girl in a choke hold, brandishing a knife. The girl's mother screamed and got slapped across the face for it. Not more than a second passed before the door slammed shut behind them, cutting off the only light. Sydney's eyes started to adjust as she wondered if Alex had witnessed any of this from his vantage point in the car.

The girl was dragged to the back stairs leading to the smaller gyms on top. She struggled keeping her balance to such an extent another masked man with a semiautomatic rifle grabbed her feet around the ankles, and the two of them brought the wriggling teen down into the back.

Through the glass partitions, Sydney could see two gym spaces upstairs holding people crowded together, their hands and faces plastered against the glass. On one side were the young players. In the adjacent gym were parents. Some were standing near the partition to their daughters' side, others sat stoically, and some looked down below to watch what the screaming and commotion was all about. In the middle of that crowd she noticed the unhappy face of Mrs. Beeson.

Sydney scanned the people, looking for evidence of a male figure somewhere, and sadly, found none. She located Carly sitting down nearby, her head in her hands resting over her knees.

Two metal ladders were set up under the overhang of the gyms upstairs. Near the top of the ladders, two men were wrapping something over a metal beam. Sydney's heart started racing when she realized they were duct taping something to the underside of the gym flooring. The objects were the size of a shoebox.

"Your purse," a masked man demanded. One of the men on the ladder looked across the gym and Sydney knew him as the older brother of one of her Somali players. In fact, Sydney thought most of the men were young, and now recalled seeing several of them coming by to pick up their sisters or relatives.

She handed the gym bag to him, letting go of the handles before he'd grabbed it, which sent the bag to the floor at his feet. The masked man stepped closer to Sydney, nearly touching her, his red eyes wide with fear he was desperately trying to mask. His right temple was pulsing, and she could see perspiration on his forehead and upper lip. He appeared high on some kind of stimulant.

The nearly one-foot difference in height proved a

distraction to him. He said something in an Arabic-sounding language and unzipped the bag, dumping the contents on the gym floor. He tossed the empty carcass into the corner piled high with other purses and bags.

Sydney was ordered to sit while the masked man pawed over her bag contents and spread them out over the concrete floor. She knew he was looking for her cell phone.

He was called away, but not before another guard was sent to stand over her. She was surprised they did not tie her up.

Underestimate me at your own peril.

After several minutes, the masked man returned.

He pointed to her earbud, still lodged deep, playing the Rocky theme that was perfect for her current situation. Her mind was racing what to do next, and expected to hear banging on the door from Alex's attempted entry any time. He'd know something was wrong if it was locked. But what would be her fate? The girls? Mrs. Beeson?

"My iPod," she insisted, pulling out her plug and handing it to the man so he could listen to the music. "For my workout, you understand?"

The man shouted and the boy she knew from the ladder immediately came running over. His eyes were downcast, as he realized Sydney had recognized him. There was a back and forth exchange between the two of them, and the boy gave her the command, "He wants your cell. He knows it's not an iPod. You don't want to play tricks with him. Very bad man, understand?"

Sydney figured that was all he could say. She took her phone off the armband and handed it to the younger man, with the ear bud still dangling. The bud was removed and the Rocky music blared from the microphone, reverberating throughout the gym. This seemed to irritate the masked man and she worried he'd destroy it. It was tossed into a box outside the office doorway with several others.

She glanced up at the group of girls and the relative of the boy was not among them, nor did there appear to be any from their immigrant family. She wanted to ask him why they were doing this, but knew she wouldn't get anything satisfactory. At least the girls were relatively calm, although several were quietly crying or hugging one another. She was grateful they could not see what must surely be two explosive devices hanging in the metal frame of the structure, right below them.

The younger man translated several bursts of language.

"He says our leader wants to use you as a hostage negotiator. If everyone cooperates, there will be no loss of life."

Sydney could tell he was lying.

An even shorter man came from Mrs. Beeson's office. He had a cash box, a couple of computers and some Beach Inc. sweatshirts in his arms. The masked man pushed Sydney in the direction of the office and she complied, but her anger was coming to a full boil.

"What would Alex do? How can I get a message to him?"

She heard lecturing coming from upstairs as one of the attackers said in perfect English, "You will cooperate or you all will die. I promise you that. You do as I say, make no problem for us, and you may live."

Response to the man's words was immediate. There was collective moaning and sniffles as the young players began to understand the danger they were in, and they began to panic. Their mothers huddled in small groups, whispering.

Just as Sydney entered the doorway and was pushed into Mrs. Beeson's rolling office chair, she remembered her Apple Watch, and understood she had the power to text. The other thing that made her happy was the fact that Mrs. Beeson always had a loaded gun under papers in the locked file cabinet. If she could find her key, there might be a way to defend herself, Sydney thought. But how could she defend herself against so many men? And how many of the girls or mothers would be injured or worse if she tried something bold?

But she knew she couldn't just sit idly by and allow the standoff to continue.

On the desk and side table were several white vests with multiple pockets sewn into them, like a fisherman's sport vest, except these pockets were jammed with small white plastic bags. It didn't take much imagination to understand that vests like this, with wires connecting the bags, were made for a suicide bomber.

A clean-shaven unmasked man walked into the office and greeted her with an almost flirtatious smile. He appeared very Westernized, and he was sporting an expensive haircut. His cultured English told her he'd been well-educated. She recognized him as the one shouting instructions to the girls above. He picked up a vest from the pile, extended his arms to Sydney, and placed it over her neck and shoulders. It was heavy.

"I am sorry, but you must wear this. But you won't be the only one," he said as he tenderly pulled her ponytail from her collar.

He smoothed the canvas material over her fleece jacket, lingering a bit too long over her breasts. He placed his palms at her upper shoulders and smoothed down over her arms.

He wore expensive cologne. His well-polished shoes looked as out of place here as he did.

"Why? Why are you doing this?"

He shrugged, then pointed to her vest. "That's a good look for you."

"Why?" Sydney insisted. She hated the man and her odds. Playing with the lives of innocent children enjoying their freedoms. Who was he to take all that away? She wasn't afraid to let him see her disgust for him.

"What is it you do here?"

"I'm a coach."

"Oh, so I think maybe you are the coach everyone talks about."

"Yes, I've coached girls from your family, perhaps. I'm doing it because it's the right thing to do."

"This I respect. But surely you understand there is a war going on."

"Not here."

"You are wrong, coach. You take away our way of life. We do the same to you. You kill women and children—"

"Because you hide amongst them."

He laughed. "Why, you don't believe we have wives and girlfriends? Children of our own?"

"You drag them into your filthy war."

"Coach, you are an ignorant woman. You should be duct taped. You should learn to have respect for those who have been trained properly. This is what's wrong with your country. You listen to too many women."

Sydney bolted out of the chair. She knew she only had one chance to get this asshole, because if she failed she would be duct taped there, perhaps for the rest of her life.

Caught off guard, he wasn't prepared for the kick Sydney delivered to his groin, but since she was wearing only flip flops, it didn't do the damage she'd hoped. He groaned and bent over, then turned and gave her a backhand to the left side of her face. She heard a crack, and knew he'd probably shattered her cheekbone. She screamed as loud as she could as a warning. She heard answering cries from upstairs.

The noise brought the other men. They were ordered to hold her down with force as her vest was removed with near delicacy.

"You stupid fool," the unmasked attacker spat out. "You nearly sent us all up to Allah."

"Isn't that what you want?" Her lips felt numb and the sputtering of blood sent droplets flying like tiny magnets, depositing themselves on the man's expensive shirt, slacks and pullover sweater.

She was brought a wet towel and a bottled water for her face. The leader received a cell phone call and went into the main gym area to seek privacy.

Temporarily, Sydney was left alone. She was satisfied they didn't notice that she also had an Apple Watch on her, and with that she could text Alex.

She extended her fingers under the sleeve of her left hand, which had the watch on it, and felt the tiny divots for the keypad on her sport model. She wasn't sure how close she came, hoping it wasn't all gibberish, but she attempted to text,

SOS Alex. Suicide bombers have everyone held hostage. Help.

She could tell the text went through because she heard a tiny swooshing sound and then a short vibration on her wrist. She hoped to God it was the right number.

Her thumbnail clicked off the sound so the attackers didn't catch on.

She shouted out to one of the attackers outside, asking to use the restroom. The younger boy walked into the office and denied her request, "You pee here if you need to." He pointed to the corner of the office, where a metal wastebasket stood.

They finally tied her to a chair with duct tape secured around her ankles and wrists. Mr. Cleancut poked his head in the doorway. "You will become famous now, Coach. Get yourself ready, say your prayers. If you do a good job, perhaps you'll survive this." He stepped inside the office, leaning closer to her and whispered, "In my country, I would have celebrated slitting your throat and watching you bleed all over yourself."

They both left the room, closing the door behind them.

SYDNEY COULD STAND with the chair strapped to her. She walked herself near the bookkeeper's desk and found scissors in the top drawer. She tried to finger them, but they slipped from her hand and dropped to the floor.

Damn it.

She eyed the telescoping back scratcher next, but ruled it out as not helpful at all.

She heard voices come near the doorway, so she kicked the scissors further under the desk, and headed back to her corner, still very much attached to the chair.

The man with the expensive cologne came into the room first.

"What is your name?"

"Sydney. S-Sydney Robinson,"

"Well, Miss Sydney Robinson, lets see how skilled you are in negotiations. I am going to dial a local TV station, you will tell them who you are, and where you are. You will not leave anything out, but only when I give you the sign that it is okay to do so. Can you do this?"

Sydney nodded her head, but kept her evil eye on

him for emphasis.

"Good." The man put his hand on his heart. "My name is Youssef. I am a messenger from God."

Sydney tried not to react. She was getting adjusted to her situation. It had been over twenty minutes since she'd walked into the gym and still there had been no knock on the door. No attempts to contact her. She hoped Alex would locate the authorities.

Youssef was not wearing a vest, like some of the others had begun to put on. Then she recalled the white vans outside the gym.

They're going to take some of us somewhere! But there wasn't enough room for everyone.

Sydney inhaled and drew courage from the satisfaction of knowing they had other plans than to just blow up the gym and everyone in it. They had enough room for maybe thirty of the girls or mothers. Perhaps they'd leave the others alone. She needed to know what his timetable and plans were.

But before she could ask Youssef, everyone left her alone again and gathered outside the doorway, joining arms over their shoulders. They spoke softly. It wasn't a meeting.

It was a farewell.

She couldn't text Alex, and panic set in as she realized the phone call to the TV station was probably just to draw news crews for publicity. She could tell, as

Youssef handed out the remaining vests, none of them were going to survive.

She struggled with the duct tape, trying to dislodge it from her wrists, and ankles. Her strong leg muscles worked hard, and finally, she was able to free one ankle. She extended her toes and slid the scissors closer toward her. She balanced the tool on the inset of her shoe, bringing it up to her lap. She tried to maneuver the blade but was unable to have it reach any tape to cut.

She was getting frustrated and needed to calm herself. As a brief reminder, her stomach lurched and she resigned herself to wait until they asked her to phone the TV station. That's when she'd make her last stand.

Then she noticed a piece of the metal trim had been dislodged from Mrs. Beeson's desk top, probably from the scuffle with Youssef. It was sufficiently sharp to use as a knife. She turned around in her chair and rubbed up and down until one wrist and then the other was freed.

She quickly undid her other ankle.

The men were still occupied outside. She fired off a text to Alex.

"They are preparing to end us all. Must hurry."
"On it. I got help. Location?"
"They're in the center. There are 8. Vests."
"Bomb vests? Hostages?"
"Yes. All upstairs, except me. In ofc down. Hurry."
"Dive under a desk and wait. Lock yourself in?"

"Yes."

She moved toward the door, but her actions drew the attention of one of the men, who spotted her through the door's window, and raised his weapon. She got behind Mrs. Beeson's large wooden desk just as the room was filled with splinters from the rounds the semiautomatic made. She didn't have a chance to lock the door and knew they'd be on top of her any second. She was defenseless. Mrs. Beeson's gun was in the lower locked file drawer, and she had no key.

Damn.

She heard the girls screaming upstairs as there were more weapons fired. Smoke started to fill the room. Sydney held her breath for as long as she could, but then she was forced to inhale the smoke fumes and it made her cough. She was getting dizzy and sick to her stomach again.

When would the man spray the room with gunfire again? Would he figure out she was behind the desk and come for her? She heard the gun go off, but not in her direction. She knew it would be very soon now, and she was on borrowed time.

Would this be the last of anything she would hear? Were they going to get her—never give her the chance to feel the life of her baby inside her? Someone would tell him. And then he'd know. But he'd hear it from a policeman, or a counselor, and not from her lips.

Everything she'd always wanted was being taken

away from her.

And then she heard the most wonderful sound in the whole world. The man she loved was shouting her name over and over again.

The happy shock of his voice made it so she couldn't move. And then his face was in front of hers.

"Did they hurt you?"

"No."

"Are you sure?"

She tried to think. "I'm not sure. H-he hit me. Can you check?"

He was on his knees in front of her. "Your face is bruised, but looks okay. You can come out now, sweetheart. Zak and the guys got here just in time, or I was going in alone. But we got the bad guys, Sydney. You helped us save everyone."

His large dark eyes scanned her body as she huddled under the desk. She began to shake. Her vision was suddenly blurry as hot tears streamed down her cheeks. The salty tears stung on one side.

"It's okay," he said as he pulled her towards him, still on his knees. "You're okay, Sydney." He rocked her from side to side gently. "Everything's okay now. I'm here, and you're safe. I'm not leaving."

She pulled back and examined his face. "Never?"

"Well, you know, go to work, but I don't want to leave you alone. I would not be able to live with myself if something happened to you, Sydney. My place is here. I'm going to stay here."

"So no Team 6?"

"Not yet, sweetheart. Maybe someday. Not now."

"You sure?"

"Positive." He gently took her hands in his. "Come on out of your cave. Let's see how you are."

She let him lead her to a standing position. A new wave of nausea hit her. He brought the metal waste-basket over for her, but she stubbornly willed the nausea away.

"Those flashbombs are nasty stuff, but not lethal. Nothing to make you sick. But they're nasty."

"Good."

She collapsed into him. The one-eyed man she'd met in San Diego who helped set up her date with Alex was in the doorway. He had two other men with him.

"Alex, we've called the fire department and cops. Everyone's okay. They didn't hurt anyone, and no one's missing."

"Hear that?"

She nodded, then buried her head in his chest. Alex whispered to his friends, "We'll be out in a second. She's in a bit of shock."

His warm body against hers was what she'd wanted to feel. She knew she needed to stay calm, for the baby.

OMG! The baby!

He was saying things to the top of her head while letting his strong fingers give her a firm neck massage. She heard him say, "I thought I'd lost you today. I never want to feel that way again. Can you see yourself married to a sailor? Would you do me the honor?"

She inhaled his words, letting them wash through her as he held her trembling body. It wasn't what she'd expected on a day with all sorts of other plans. Savoring the moment, she was willingly stringing it out for as long as she could make it. Because now she was going to have to say something that might change everything. And she'd have to make that okay, whatever the outcome.

"Sydney? Did you hear me? I want you to be my wife."

After just a few more seconds of being nourished in his arms, she was ready. "You need to know something first."

"No, baby. No bad news. We'll talk about all this tomorrow." He hugged her tighter. "Only good things today. Tell me you'll think about it. Promise me?"

She separated from him enough to look directly into his eyes.

"It isn't bad news, Alex. Not bad at all. What I mean is yes, Alex, I'll marry you. But there's something else you need to know first."

"Whatever it is, we'll get through it. We'll overcome anything you and I."

That made her smile. *How in the world does one overcome a lifetime of raising a child?*

"What is it, Sydney? Tell me."

She splayed her fingers over his warm chest, feeling the solid wall that was his body—willing and capable of shielding her, protecting her, risking his life for her. This wasn't going to be anything he'd trained for.

"Sweet Alex, what I wanted to say and was afraid to tell you was, I'm pregnant."

CHAPTER 28

A LEX COULDN'T BELIEVE what she'd just said. Sirens were going off as the rescue squads arrived. Zak and the other two Team guys had backed away, giving them the privacy they obviously needed. With a tornado of activity going on all around them, her tear-streaked face still smiled back at him. And yes, she looked a tiny bit worried about his reaction. So he'd have to tell her something.

He didn't have to dig very far. He knew it just as soon as she said it. He was overjoyed with her news.

"Baby, that's the best thing I've heard all day, honest to God."

He felt her knees buckle. Her eyes closed as she collapsed into him.

"Sweetheart, are you okay?"

A heavyset, graying female paramedic rushed into the destroyed office, surveyed the scene, saw Sydney's weakened state, and ordered Alex to put her down on the gurney brought in by her skinny male partner behind her.

"She's—she's pregnant," he told the paramedic.

"Gotcha. Hon, you get hurt anywhere? They do anything to you or you fall, sweetheart?"

Sydney tried to sit up and was gently restrained.

"Hold on there. We just want to check you out." She glanced up at Alex. "You got some water so I don't have to get it?"

As he maneuvered around the gurney, Zak threw him a fresh bottle. He heard Sydney say, "There's some—oh wait, my bag is over there on the pile."

"No, he's already got you some fresh water, sugar. You just relax and let this nice-looking young man take care of you. It looks like he's the right kinda medicine for you!"

Sydney smiled, and then began to laugh. "He sure is," she said after she gave him a bashful expression. Alex lifted her head up and placed the cold water to her mouth. A bit spilled down her neck, and he dabbed it with the blanket. He set the water down on the desk nearby, and then grasped her right hand between both of his, kissing her knuckles. He had never been more proud.

"God, I can't wait until you get fat. I don't even care about the volleyball anymore. I just want to see that belly get huge, Sydney."

The paramedic's eyes sprung to mock alarm right in the middle of extracting Sydney's arm from under the soft blanket. "You hear that?" she barked.

Sydney was streaming tears, her lower lip quivering. She could barely say his name. "Alex—"

"Right here, baby." He leaned over to kiss her and she grabbed his neck, hooking it with her right arm. "Whoa! I'm not going anywhere, Sydney."

"All I can say—" the paramedic began as she pushed up Sydney's workout top, wrapped the blood pressure cuff around her left arm and began pumping. Alex glanced upward for the result. After a few seconds, she added in a whisper, "She's fine, blood pressure amazingly normal." Placing her very large hand gently against his chest, she added, "Give me a little room, sugar. There will no doubt be time for that later." She followed it up with a wink.

Alex stood straight and let the woman check Sydney's cheek, her eyes, and then she moved her head back and forth gently on the white cover. She removed her hands and adjusted the blanket. "You getting more comfortable now?"

Sydney nodded.

"Like I was sayin', this one here—he's a keeper! Any man who says something like that, you keep that man around. Don't you dare let him stray, you hear?"

Carly, Zak and the two other SEALs were chatting

in the doorway but stopped when they heard this.

"Carly!" Sydney shouted out, extending her arms wide. Her friend bolted past everyone and wrapped her arms around Sydney's upper torso.

"Oh, Sydney, you put yourself at too much risk for all of us. I don't know how you managed to get these guys here to show up, but I'm damn glad you did." She glanced between the SEALs. "Thank you all."

"So good to see you well, and the girls?" Sydney asked.

"Oh. My. God. They're going to have stories. I think the tweets have already started, once they got their cell phones back." She gave Sydney one last hug. "I need to go check on the girls." And then she left the office.

"Show's over folks," the paramedic said. None of them moved. "Oh, you must be with him." She crooked her thumb over her shoulder. "All these guys looking all kind of wonderful. Give her some space, let her catch up. Now I gotta go check on some skinny butt, anorexic teenagers. I'll be back. Don't leave with my cart, okay, darlin'?" She winked at Alex in an unabashed flirt.

She parted the wall at the doorway and then stopped, turning around, "Young lady, you remember what I told you about him. Keep him around, and I hope you have a beautiful baby. Oh, and I don't think anything busted up here," she pointed to her own cheek, "but best get an xray soon anyhow. You rest for a couple of days. Take it easy. Let this guy get all nekked and wait on you hand and foot. You make him shake that fine ass—oh yes, I saw it. You didn't think old Muriel here would notice such things, but I still do!"

When she left, the room seemed empty.

"She's right about the rest, you know," said Alex. He brought his arms around her, scooping her waist so she could feel how badly he wanted to hold her.

"The rest of what?" Sydney whispered, arching backward, her arms above her head.

"The rest. Bed rest."

"Well then that means you're gonna get lots too, Alex. I'm going to need an awful lot of tender loving care. Your very best."

"You'll have it. You'll always have it, Sydney. Forever."

He loved that her softness was coming back. The panic in her eyes was gone, the distraction, masking the hurt and pain. Girls started walking by, and he had to share her with several of them.

"Oh my God, Miss Robinson, we saw you down there, and were like, 'Oh no!! Leave her alone.' We were ready to just bust out and take over those guys, but then they started shooting!" With her braces, the enthusiastic teen was slurring her words and spitting all over everyone. She glanced over at Alex. "Is he your boyfriend?"

"No, he's my fiancé, Janine."

The girls screamed. Several jumped up and down. "Oh, that is so cool. You were saved by your fiancé. Oh my God. That is just so romantic!"

Several others had similar things to say. Zak and Kurt and Eric stood near the wall, sucking in their waists and expanding their pecs, their arms crossed, exposing a lot of ink.

After the bevy of well-wishers and mothers were gone, Alex lifted the blanket. "Come on, sweetheart. Time to get home, get showered up, and get your butt in the bed where it belongs."

She placed her arm around his shoulder and neck, and he lifted her in his arms. Out in the main gym area, several white sheets covered the bodies of the kidnappers. Two were still alive, being escorted by police. Sydney waved to one of them as they passed by. A news crew was trying to gain entry and was barred at the doorway.

"Does the investigator need to speak to me?" he asked Zak.

"Not today. I filled him in. He knows you have to take her home. You sure she doesn't need to go to the hospital?"

He turned and spat out his answer at the same time Sydney did. "No!" Then he softened. "We'll do that after she's rested up."

BACK AT HER apartment, he insisted on carrying her up the stairs. They'd retrieved her wallet at the gym along with the bag, which he'd slung over his shoulder. He unlocked the door and carried her over the threshold.

"I guess I better enjoy this while I can. I won't be able to carry you much longer, will I?"

"Oh stop it, Alex. I'm not going to get that big."

"Oh, but sweetheart, you get as big as you want. I honestly don't care."

"I'm pregnant, not fat. I won't get fat."

He set her down but couldn't keep his hands off her. "And I believe you, I honestly do! Just want you to know, Sydney, it's okay with me. We want a healthy baby. That's all that matters."

"So I guess that means skydiving tomorrow is out?"

"Absolutely it's out. After what you just went through today?"

"Well then, whatever can we do?"

"Well,"—he scratched the back of his neck—"I'm thinking of a few things we could do, once you're settled." He added, "You should take that warmup stuff off, to begin with."

"Okay. Why don't you sit right there?"

"Yes, ma'am," he said as he fell back into the easy chair.

She unzipped her top, slowly. Too slowly. She carefully revealed the yellow top he'd seen on those darned magazines. He licked his lips, suddenly parched for the taste of her. That brought a smile to her lips.

She let the top drop to the ground, then stepped out of her shoes. Next she pushed her pants down those gorgeous thighs, and then stepped out of them all together.

Her little yellow uniform was on parade as she slowly turned. The woman didn't have an extra ounce of fat anywhere. Her calves were well defined, even her toes looked sexy. She angled her hips as she presented her backside to him, the thong not covering one damn thing. Her butt cheeks were tight and compact like ripe fruit.

He was glad he never saw her play on the beach in the flesh. He'd have been so jealous, he'd have gotten into trouble. But she wore her outfit with complete confidence. Not an ounce of self-consciousness in her. She was a lean, mean spike and jumping machine. Her long muscled arms hung down gracefully at her sides, her wrists small, her cherry-red fingernails splayed out.

When she was facing him again, she slipped one strap of her top over her shoulder, then the other. The little halter top was pulled up and over her head. Her arms crossed, revealing her washboard abs. She stood with her right knee bent, her hips at an angle, her awesome form now naked from below her navel up. She threw the top at him. Hard.

That got to him. He was on his feet, pursuing her as she screamed and scampered into the bathroom, trying to close the door. He forced it open, enjoying the chase, enjoying her strength and her defiance of him. She had him wrapped around her little finger.

She turned on the shower, stepping inside with her little thong still intact. Her eyes taunted him, as if she thought the shower would make her safe. He kicked off his shoes and stepped into the stall fully clothed. Warm water drizzled down his back, soaking his shirt. He fell to his knees, almost in a beg, as he reached over with both hands and gripped the thong pulling it down her backside. As it fell to her knees, he buried his head in her crotch.

She was sweaty and salty tasting. But once he got his tongue inside, her moistness was sweet. He sucked her bud and heard her moan.

"Are you for real, Sydney? Is this all for real?"

She was backed into the corner, one foot balancing on the tiled ledge, exposing herself to him intimately. His forefinger rubbed the wet length of her slit, before he gently inserted two fingers and watched for signs this was not allowed. He bit the delicate folds of her labia and swirled his tongue over her little nub.

Quickly, she was on him, her long legs wrapped around his waist. She ripped apart his shirt, the buttons popping on the floor of the shower. She bit his nipple and then kissed up his neck. At last their mouths connected while she pulled his shirt off one shoulder and then the other.

He sat her on the ledge and removed the rest of his shirt, throwing it over the glass enclosure. He began to unbutton his wet pants, but she was suddenly on her knees, hungrily doing it for him, shedding the wet jeans to his ankles. He felt her hands inside his shorts and then they slid the elastic waistband down his thighs.

She pulled herself up on him, her powerful thigh muscles hugging his waist, as she angled and then found him at her opening.

They were face to face, the water splashing from his shoulder into her eyes. While the large droplets sluiced down between them both, she forced herself down on him as he held her buttocks, squeezing hard and pressing her deeper.

He knew he couldn't hold out long at all especially as she began riding him up and down. She increased the frequency until he could hold on no longer. She didn't stop while he pumped her full until he felt her internal twitching. She pressed herself hard against him, holding on to him with her incredibly strong arms, nearly squeezing the air right out of him.

They began the slow descent together, touching and kissing, rubbing gel on each other. She kneeled at his feet and helped him step out of his wet boxers and jeans, depositing them outside the shower door. Still on her knees, she poured the lemon-scented shower gel over his legs, smoothing his calves, knees and thighs with her delicate fingers. She washed his cock, squeezing his balls before moving up to rub gel all over his chest, down his arms, and up his neck. Then she turned him around and did the same to his back.

He turned back to face her, "I'm supposed to wait on *you*," he whispered to her wet hair.

"I know," she said, outlining his lips with her forefinger, "but I couldn't stop myself. Somehow, I'm always out of control around you."

"Me too, sweetheart."

"Promise me something."

"I promise."

"Promise me you won't be gone when our baby is born."

"Sweetheart, I can't promise that, but I'll try." He didn't want to ask, but he had to. "Are you saying you want me to get out?"

"No, Alex. That's who you are. I just want you to be there. Not on a monitor somewhere else. Don't let them take that away from us."

"It really does depend on what we get. But I won't volunteer for anything if there's a chance it will interfere. That's the best I can do. I'll work miracles to see to it that I'm there. I do promise that."

"That's good enough for me. I want you here for all the big events in my life, in our lives. In our baby's life."

"We'll find a way, Sydney. Maybe I won't re-up. Maybe I'll stay here and we'll do the winery. You can continue to coach, if you want. Or go for the AVP tour after the baby's here. Anything you want, sweetheart. What do you say?"

"If you're by my side, anything is possible, Alex. Anything."

It was his time to kneel. He kissed her firm belly, rubbing his palm over the flat, toned flesh, and whispered, "I'm your daddy. And I'll love you both forever."

The End

ABOUT THE AUTHOR

 NYT and USA Today best-selling author Sharon Hamilton's award-winning Navy SEAL Brotherhood series have been a fan favorite from the day the first one was released. They've earned her the coveted Amazon author ranking of #1 in Romantic Suspense, Military Romance and Contemporary Romance categories, as well as in Gothic Romance for her Vampires of Tuscany and Guardian Angels. Her characters follow a sometimes rocky road to redemption through passion and true love.

Her Golden Vampires of Tuscany are not like any vamps you've read about before, since they don't go to ground and can walk around in the full light of the sun.

Her Guardian Angels struggle with the human charges they are sent to save, often escaping their vanilla world of Heaven for the brief human one. You won't find any of these beings in any Sunday school class.

She lives in Sonoma County, California with her husband and two Dobermans. A lifelong organic gardener, when she's not writing, she's getting *verra*

verra dirty in the mud, or wandering Farmers Markets looking for new Heirloom varieties of vegetables and flowers.

She loves hearing from her fans:

sharonhamilton2001@gmail.com

Her website is:

www.authorsharonhamilton.com

Find out more about Sharon, her upcoming releases, appearances and news from her newsletter.

authorsharonhamilton.com/contact.php#mailing-list

Sharon's Blog:

sharonhamiltonauthor.blogspot.com

Facebook:

facebook.com/SharonHamiltonAuthor

Twitter:

@sharonlhamilton

Life is one fool thing after another.
Love is two fool things after each other.